Thanks to Elsha Tiemersma for designing the cover and to Madison Kopp for helping develop the idea!

Nonymous

Nonymous

To all the people I thought I had to lose to find myself.
I hope you're doing well.

Nonymous

Nonymous

Grade 8: Marnie

Nonymous

Corrina Murphy is perhaps the coolest person who's ever existed and I'm lucky enough to be the only one who's realized that so far.

I was quite literally made for Cory. I would have probably been made eventually without her, but this me—the one born April 6th, 2001—only came to be because my mum thought that it would be fun to be pregnant at the same time as Cory's. I've revolved around Cory since before conception, so falling in love with her was always inevitable. She was my first peer then first friend then first soulmate. My first playdate and sleepover. We've been a million other firsts too: swimming lessons, hikes, recitals, school dances. She's been there for first skinned knees and lost teeth and periods. But not this first. This time, she can't be.

"Who?" She whispers for the tenth time in no more than twenty seconds. We're crouched together under the slide, hiding from all the commotion behind us. Jackson Walker's hosting a grade-wide pool party tomorrow so we'll all see each other again soon, but the last day of school is apparently such a momentous occasion to everyone else that our teachers let us out before the final bell so that we can say goodbye to the other two grade eight classes. It's no big deal to us, though. We've never needed the rest of them.

Cory's fingers are still wrapped around mine from when she'd caught on to how desperate I was to not be involved in any of the hugging, crying, and mobbing and whisked me away. Her nails are covered in sparkling, chipped purple polish.

I blush. "No one. Pretend I didn't say anything."

"Marn!" Her knee whacks against mine. "You can't do that! I won't be able to stop wondering about it all summer."

I'd fallen into a trap. She'd made some comment about how I was graduating without having my first crush yet and I'd been so used to correcting her on impulse that I'd accidentally said a bit too much of the truth.

I stare at the woodchips. Un-wedge one from the grooves of my sneaker. "Just some girl I met last summer."

This time, it's her palm that hits my knee. "Last summer!"

"It wasn't a big deal!" I make myself laugh. "She didn't even know I existed. I would've told you if it was an actual thing."

"You still should have! I told you about—"

"I know," I stop her. If I have to listen to her list off every boy I've ever helped her chase after ever since she decided that boys were worthy of chasing back in sixth grade, it will destroy me. "But you were on a whole other continent. It's not like you could have helped."

She sighs, leaning her head against my shoulder. "Next time, okay?" She reaches a purple speckled nail up in front of my face. "I wanna know about girl stuff."

"Sure," I link my finger through hers. "Of course." I see my chance. I move to sit across from her and make myself look into her eyes—gray. She calls them blue, but she's wrong—before speaking. "I need us to make an oath though."

Her expression goes serious. She nods once before instantly digging through my bag for our supplies.

"We're not changing, okay?" I say. "Because of high school or boys or girls or... whatever. We're staying exactly like this forever."

She arches an eyebrow. "Fourteen and single?"

"Cory." I kick her shoe.

"Fine." She smiles, unwrapping a HunGum and handing it to me. They're quite possibly the worst candy ever made—jujubes half-hazardly dunked in honey to create a monstrosity impossible to unstick from both the wrapper or your molars. They also used to be the only thing cheap enough for us to buy from the corner story ever day when we first started getting allowances back when we were eight though, so they've become a ritual staple.

"I promise," Cory holds out her free pinky. "that we'll never, ever change no matter what or else all of my candy and toys will immediately go to Marina Accardi."

"I promise that we'll never ever change no matter what or else all of my candy and toys will immediately go to Corrina Isabella Murphy," I recite back.

We pop the HunGums into our mouths and repeat the oath once more through fused together teeth. And then, it's done. We're infinite. We're immortal. We're this forever and always.

And maybe there's a part of me that will always hope that we won't be. Maybe there's a part of me that already regrets making the promise. But if we can never be anything more, I'll be happy with an eternity of exactly this.

Corrina Murphy is perhaps the coolest person who's ever existed, I'm in love with her, and she likes a new boy every month. Corrina Murphy is absolutely the coolest person I've ever known, I'm in love with her, and no matter how much I wish it wasn't true, I already know that we won't end up together.

Nonymous

Nonymous

Grade 9: Cory

Nonymous

Nonymous

Chapter 1

I've been in love with Marnie Accardi since sixth grade.

We'd hiked this trail by our apartment that we'd both been in millions of times before, but never alone together. It felt daring, somehow. Being alone with her and nothing but trees. It was barely a hike (we'd have to drive to get to the kind of terrain that would actually count as that and the whole point of that day was us proving that we were independent) but we still went to the highest point we could find and I swear that in that moment, just for that one day, the ground seemed miles beneath us. Marnie had stuffed a blanket into her bag because Marnie has always been infinitely better at preparing for stuff than I've ever been, and we spread it out to look at the sky.

Marnie was the one who'd suggested cloud watching. She was always full of stuff like that. Marnie wasn't Marnie if she wasn't approaching every social interaction with at least three back up plans. It was the first time that we'd tried that particular activity though so while I leaned back and pointed out rabbits and snow cones and that one that looked weirdly like our fourth-grade gym teacher screaming at someone, she was just quiet.

"What about you?" I asked. "What do you see?"

Marnie gets these lines on her nose when she's thinking. She does a lot of that. I'm pretty sure she'll have permanent wrinkles before we reach twenty. Her nose scrunched up. Her eyes squinted. She waited another long moment before just saying, "clouds."

I laughed and started to sit up, but she grabbed my arm. "I've got this," she said. "keep telling me what you see. I'll catch on eventually."

So, I pointed out animals and buildings and phallic symbols until eventually she said, "I see that one!" with the kind of excitement in her voice that would make it impossible to not want to look at her just for a chance of stealing some of it for yourself.

Nonymous

When I did, her eyes were closed. Not tight, just gentle. Not a wrinkle in sight. The grin didn't leave her face when she asked "what else?"

I never called her out on lying. I've never called her out on it at all because I'm pretty sure she wasn't. It was stupid, but nothing could have convinced me that Marnie wasn't staring at exactly what I was describing against the underside of her eyelids.

"Lion," I supplied. "See the mane?" But I didn't see that one either. I watched her think and smile and nod. I watched her hair in the grass and the breath in her chest.

"What else?"

Marnie has a single freckle right on the upper left part of her top lip. I've always had way more than her (I get tons in the summers) but even though I'd felt mine hundreds of times already and knew that they were always smooth, I ran a thumb over my wrist, wondering if hers would feel distinct against my skin.

I almost tested it. Not kissing her (I still don't know if I wanted to kiss her), just touching it. I held my breath and reached out a finger to stroke her lip, just so I could stop wondering. But then she repeated "what else?" and the hot breath on my knuckles sent shivers all the way up my arm so I flipped back over to look at the sky so quickly that I had a bruise on my elbow that would last days.

"Snow cone." It was a reused offering, but my heart was beating too quickly to focus on anything else.

"Didn't we do that one that one already?" Marnie asked, like nothing was happening. Because to her, nothing was.

"Oh."

In that moment, everything had felt so clear. There was me and Marnie and the sky and this new nervousness that definitely shouldn't have taken up residence in my chest. In that moment I knew without a shadow of a doubt that I was in love with her and maybe that wasn't even when all that nervousness had first started, but it was the first time I was able to name it. But then a boy called me funny a couple of weeks later and set so many butterflies loose within me that I was convinced I was about to vomit and things felt a lot messier. There are words for people who like multiple genders. There were back then too and I probably could have found them, if I'd wanted to. Both of our moms had always been so ridiculously supportive about Marnie liking girls that I was pretty sure they were just waiting for me to come clean too. But I also knew that getting nauseous about a boy so insignificant that I no longer even remember his name would be a lot less difficult to deal with than liking Marnie, so I decided that if there were words for whatever I felt for her, I didn't want to know them.

    But, in that moment, I knew. More than I've ever known anything. I stared at the sky until my eyes unfocused and my vision went blurry. Until it was nothing more than undefined swirls of white and blue. I threw out noun after noun even though I couldn't make out any of the shapes either at that point just to give Marnie something to pull up in her brain.

    We weren't staring at the same sky. One of us wasn't even looking at it. But we were experiencing each other's and that was somehow better, I think.

And now, I'm on a plane. Clouds look different from up here. They're only actually clear when you're far away so I'm not thinking about shapes. But I am thinking about her.

    I think the distance might help there too. Every summer I leave for two months and return back certain that I'm in love with Marnie. I might get crushes on other people when I physically see them every day, but Marnie's the only one that ever actually sticks. This summer was different though, more significant. This time I'm no longer some little kid trying to figure out the difference between love and friendship. We're about to be high schoolers now and I'm not doing that without her knowing, for better or for worse.

    We'll land. I might chicken out from marching right over to her apartment because I've already been freaking myself out every time I've thought about texting her all summer, but I'll see her tomorrow morning.

Marnie's a creature of habit. It's the only reason I've ever been anything close to productive. She was the kind of kid who'd schedule every minute of playdates weeks in advance, I was the kind who'd ignore all of our plans no matter how fun they sounded, stuff her face with sand, and then wonder why her stomach was suddenly cramping.

Marnie's a creature of habit so even if my brain keeps being stupid and chickening out, I'll see her tomorrow morning and then I know I'll tell her no matter how nervous it might make me feel because I might actually explode if I don't.

First days of school go like this: three to five texts the night before confirming whose apartment we're meeting at (even though it always ends up being mine), two to three again the next morning, then a knock on my door right as the clock turns to whatever specific minute we've decided on that my mom will inevitably have to answer because I'll inevitably be late. All I have to do this time is not be. I'll set a dozen alarms to counteract the jetlag and be exactly on time which means we'll get to school early because Marnie always makes sure to account for all of my inevitabilities.

I'm going to make sure I have time to tell her.

Except we land and I turn my service back on as quickly as I can, but there are no texts waiting for me.

I could reach out first. Normally, I'd just reach out first. But nothing about any of this feels normal.

Mom calls Pia in the taxi on the way home. She always does (Pia's terrified of flying and always convinces herself we've died in some kind of firey explosion) and I try to casually lean closer as if I'll hear Marnie breathing through the phone. They must be home together. Marnie would never risk being tired for the first day of high school which means that they're in the same apartment right now and she probably hears our moms on the phone and knows that I'm back. I check my phone. Still nothing.

16

We get back to our apartment and there's still nothing and I unpack half my stuff (and throw the other half onto my closet floor) and there's still nothing and when I lie down to try to go to sleep, there's still nothing there. Finally, I cave. One text. Two words.

i'm back

Another two.

730 tomorrow?

No response. I could get up. I could storm down the hall and slam my fist against her door until it'd be impossible to ignore me. But that's not how this was supposed to work.

I was going to get back home and she'd be waiting right there, somehow in my apartment already. I somehow wouldn't be surprised because that's where she belongs. I'd say something rambly (probably "hey, sorry I didn't text you as much as usual this summer. I was too busy dealing with the fact that I'm pretty sure I'm in love with you") and she'd say something equally rambly but slightly more intelligent back (probably "totally fine, I'm also in love with you" except she'd use at least one word that I wouldn't be one hundred percent sure on the definition of) and then everything would be perfect.

I've liked boys and girls (or girl, but so intensely that it has to still count) and pretty much every personality type at some point or another, but none of it's felt like Marnie. That's supposed to mean something. That's supposed to be proof that we're soulmates. Inevitable since birth. But maybe I was wrong. How can I possibly pretend to know anything about destiny when I don't even know what's going on with my own sexuality yet? Maybe we won't end up together.

I set my alarm for six, just in case.

Chapter 2

I've been late to school before, but it's never felt this unfair. By the time I finally give up on waiting for Marnie, I've been awake for hours already. I'll have to sprint to even have a chance at making it to first period in time which means I'll be all sweaty and gross (which isn't exactly the first impression you want to go for when you know everyone will already be hype focusing on your weight and perceived lack of athleticism), and I'm not even well rested enough for it to be worth it.

She still hasn't texted.

That's okay. Whatever's going on with Marnie, she'll have to face me soon enough. We made sure our schedules lined up and Marnie would never miss a class just because of some weird sudden grudge. I've never done the first day of school without her before, but I walked to middle school dozens of times on my own so I can do it today and then everything will go back to normal.

I only make it to the parking lot before I almost get hit by a car.

It's probably more embarrassing that it's not the first time that that's happened to me. I'm pretty sure everyone new that moves into our apartment complex gets warned about it when they sign the leases at this point.

"Watch out for that 'bigger' girl with the frizzy blonde hair. Especially if she's wearing headphone."

I've always had this nasty habit of getting so lost in my head that I forget the rest of the world exists. Jumping back onto the sidewalk when a car suddenly materializes out of nowhere is practically second nature at this point.

A horn honks. I know the near collision was almost definitely my fault, but adults normally at least have the decency to pretend it wasn't.

"Corrina!"

I freeze. I try to subtly turn to hide my face, but I've already been spotted.

"Corinna!" Mrs. DeLuca calls again. "Are you just leave for school now?"

I try to hide my grimace as I turn to face her. I have nothing personal against Mrs. Deluca. According to my mom, she's a perfectly lovely person. It's not her fault that she birthed a demon.

"Yeah," I smile. "Slept in."

"Need a ride?"

I look past her. Gabe (the demon in question) is staring pointedly out the other window, pretending I don't exist.

"That's fine." Pretending to smile for much longer might make me vomit. "I like walking."

Mrs. Deluca frowns. "You're going to be late. We probably will be too, and I doubt you can outrun a car." She nudges Gabe's shoulder. "Someone forgot to print out his schedule and didn't realize that he'd need it until we were already halfway there."

"I don't—"

"Get in the car before we're both late." Gabe grumbles.

I sigh. I open the back door and use it as a cover to fix my smile.

"What classes do you have, Cory?" Mrs. Deluca prompts. "Maybe you and Gabe'll have a few together."

I swallow. Mrs. Deluca might very well be a perfectly lovely person, but she's also painfully oblivious. It's less than a ten-minute drive to the school, but it still feels like an eternity.

By the time we get to school, the bell's already finished ringing. The final few notes of *O'Canada* fade away as I pull the door open. Mrs. Deluca left right after dropping us off in the parking lot, so I don't bother pretending to hold it for Gabe. Marnie might be acting weird today, but her enemies are my enemies until the end of time. I pull out my schedule to find my first period, but the footsteps behind me don't fade away.

"Stop following me." I don't turn around.

Instead, Gabe speeds up to fall into pace beside me. "You don't own the school, Cory. Just trying to get to class."

I keep walking. So does he.

I sigh. "French?" I check.

He nods once.

Marnie will hate that. High school always felt so much bigger whenever we talked about it. Like everyone we didn't like from middle school would magically disappear the second we got there. At least we'll have each other. Because she's obviously saved me a seat. Marnie's not a petty enough person to risk sitting with a stranger all semester just because she decided to ditch me today.

There's talking inside of room 204 as we approach it, but it falls silent when Gabe pulls the door open. A pencil-thin faux-red head stares at us. She does not look pleased.

She says something in French. I absolutely do not know what she's saying in French. I stand there like an idiot.

"Désolé," Gabe pushes past me. I feel embarrassingly proud to have recognized a single word even though everything they say to each other after that goes completely over my head. I'm half decent at French in writing where I can reread the words I've missed, but out loud, It's impossible.

Gabe eventually moves to talk a seat which means I'm probably supposed to too. I stay frozen. I scan the room over and over again, but there's no Marnie.

My chest suddenly feels heavy. Marnie's a creature of habit and she's been breaking every single one of them and I never even once considered that something could have happened to her. But my mom talked to Pia last night. She would have told her if something had happened. They would have told me because Marnie and I aren't even supposed to breath without the other person knowing about it so if something's happened to her, they would have known that I was supposed to be there for it.

The french teacher keeps saying something in a language I can barely decipher even when my brain isn't screaming at me. I open my mouth to respond before realizing that I have no idea what I'd be responding to. Gabe pushes back the chair beside him and it screeches so loudly that I'm momentarily back in my body. I sheepishly walk over to accept the seat and class resumes.

I know I'm already probably on thin ice with the teacher, but I need to know. I slip my phone out of my pocket, hide it under the desk, and text her.

me: *where r u?*
me: *r u ok?*
me: *did something happen?*

It's not until my phone buzzes on the way to my next period that I realize: there weren't any other free seats in French class. They weren't expecting Marnie either.

marnie: *I'm fine.*

I should feel relieved (I am relieved, partially), but I also know what it means. If Marnie's fine, the only explanation left for her sudden absence is that we aren't.

I was supposed to have every class with Marnie this semester. It turns out, I only have one.

I want to talk to her in gym. I need to talk to her in gym. Talking to her has quite literally been all I've been thinking about for months now. But she's somehow already befriended half of the class which makes no sense because I'm supposed to be the extroverted one but she's smiling and laughing with people I don't even know and it's all too big and daunting and different so I say nothing to any of them.

I don't know when she slipped away, but she must have. The only place she could have done it was in the change room. When I get home and chuck my bag onto the bed, a ziplock full of jelly beans falls out of the side pocket.

I just stare at it on the carpet as if that'll make it disappear. Then, with shaky hands, I undo the zipper. A single teddy bear stares up at me, a piece of paper tucked into his tie.

Sorry.

I unfold it expecting an explanation or accusation or at least something, but all it says is *I think we should take a break from each other for a bit.*

I crumple up the note and toss it to the floor. I pick up the bear and stare into his dull eyes.

If Marnie thinks she can get rid of me with a note, then she never knew me at all.

Chapter 3

"Marnie!" I pound my fist against her door. "Marnie, open the freaking—"

It opens.

Her hair's in French braids. It's the first thing I notice because Marnie isn't supposed to know how to do that because I intentionally kept putting off teaching her to give myself an excuse to always be the one to braid it. She frowns at me, leaning out to look down the hall in both directions. "You didn't have to scream," she says. "People might—"

I throw the bag of jellybeans at her face.

Marnie catches them. She slips them into her pocket. "You got my note, then."

"I... what the hell, Marnie! You don't get to—"

"Please don't hate me," she whispers.

I freeze. Marnie is the kind of person who gets quiet when she's upset. I'm the kind who sets herself on fire. I take a breath. "Can I come in?"

She chews at her lip, looking into the hall again.

I sigh. "You don't get to friendship dump me with a note then not explain why, Marn."

"I don't want the moms to know," she says. "They won't..."

"Is Pia home?"

"Not yet, she—"

I push past her. "Then you'd better hurry up and explain why you suddenly decided to suck."

I sit on her couch. She sits on her other couch. We're not supposed to be this far away from each other.

We're both silent. We're not supposed to be that either.

I tap my foot against her coffee table. "Did something happen this summer?" I check. "Are you—"

"I'm fine," she says. "Great, actually. Better than... I'm really, really good."

"That's good."

"What about you? Was your summer umm..."

"Normal. Boring."

She just keeps nodding.

I sigh. "What—"

"I have a girlfriend!" She blurts out.

I dig my nails into the couch cushion. "Good," I lie. "That's great." I pretend. "Who—"

"Isabelle Ryan? You don't know her."

"Oh." I'm supposed to ask more, but my chest is suddenly impossibly tight. I don't know what I thought was going to happen. I was never really going to come back and announce that I liked her. I tell myself I'm going to every year and then never see it through. It wasn't fair to expect her to just wait around for me forever while I figure out whatever the hell's going on with my sexuality.

It wasn't fair to expect her to wait, but I still needed her to.

"So, I've been hanging out with her a lot," she continues. "Obviously. And her friends. They're..."

"Did Isabelle tell you that you couldn't hang out with me anymore?"

Marnie's eyes go wide. Brown. Like honey. "What? No, she'd never—"

"Because if some girl's telling you—"

"I'm allowed to make decisions on my own!"

I just stare.

She realizes that she's stood up then starts to lower herself back down to the couch before setting her jaw and getting up again. "I love you," she says.

It's my in. "Then—"

24

"I love you," she repeats. Bolder. Sharper. Like someone not entirely Marnie. "But I'm... I've never had friends outside of you, Cory. I've never had anything outside of you."

"That's because we don't need anyone else," I remind her. "We're—"

"You get to have things though," she stops me. "You get to join teams and clubs and go to different countries and—"

"I've never told you not to do any of that," I remind her. "I'm constantly trying to get you to join things with me."

"I know!" she says. "I know! I just... I'm tired of not getting to have a life outside of you. I want to see... I liked this summer. I liked... I think I started figuring out who I am this summer and I don't want that to stop just—"

"I've never tried to make you be anything less than yourself."

"I was supposed to take drama," she says. "And business. I filled my whole schedule with things I didn't even—"

"I would have done music with you," I remind her. "I offered."

She smiles a little, but there are tears in her eyes.
Brown. Like honey.

"You would have been awful at that, Cor. Probably would've flunked out."

I nod. "I know. I still would've—"

"You didn't do anything wrong," she stops me. "I promise. But I'm... I don't think I can do anything right, when you're there? It's too easy to just let you decide everything for me and I can't... just one semester, okay? One semester so I can practice being on my own a bit more, then—"

"You don't get to decide when we're allowed to be friends, Marnie."

"I know. But—"

"I'm supposed to what? Wait around until you decide I'm allowed to talk to you again then pretend none of this ever happened? I'm not doing that!"

She sniffles. "I love you," she repeats, as if that fixes everything. As if that makes any of this okay. "And if you love me, you'll—"

I feel the spark again, just beneath my ribs. She doesn't get to do that. She doesn't get to throw me away and then say that I'm the one who doesn't love us enough as if she isn't the only thing I'm ever thinking about. I stand up. "It's not fair to ask me to wait."

"I know, but—"

"I'm not going to, Marnie. If you get rid of me now..."

I let the sentence hang in the air because she's not supposed to let me finish it, but instead she just nods.

"Okay. I'm... that's fair." She pulls the jellybeans back out of her pocket. "Here, I—"

"We said all of it."

"What?"

"All the toys and candy. This isn't all of it."

She frowns. "That's just a stupid little ritual we made up when we were—"

"You said all of it." It's an unreasonable ask. It's an impossible ask. But Marnie is good at doing things by the book so when she realizes that she can't possibly live up to her end of the oath, she'll have to unbreak it.

She wipes at her face as she stands up. "Okay."

And then, ten minutes later, she's back with a garbage bag of stuffed animals and chocolate bars. She holds it out to me. "Here."

I have no use for any of it, but I take it anyway. It feels good to be taking something from her too.

"This is it then?" I check. "Seriously?"

She's quiet.

"Seriously, Marnie. Last chance to stop—"

"I have to," she whispers. "I'm sorry. I love you."

"I really thought you did."

The door catches on the bag on the way out and doesn't close quite loudly enough. I reopen it just to slam it more effectively but then I accidentally see her and she's Marnie and she's crying and it has always been my job to keep that from happening.

I sigh, holding out the bag. "Keep it. I'm being stupid."

She shakes her head. "No, I... I promised. You can—"

"Marn," I walk over to hand it to her. "Keep it, okay?" I squeeze her shoulder.

"I love you," she whispers.

It doesn't feel like it. It really doesn't feel like it. But she's Marnie and she's crying so I pull her against my chest. "Okay, I know. You too, alright? Everything's going to be alright."

"You should go," she manages.

So I do. I don't get to yell. I don't get to slam the door. I walk two doors over to my apartment, double check that Mom hasn't gotten home earlier then normal, and let myself fall apart.

Chapter 4

I'm not pathetic enough to hope that the pounding at my door the next morning is Marnie. I know it won't be. Marnie's not a fan of confrontation or noise.

I am pathetic enough to know that if I thought it was her, I would open it in a heartbeat.

I finger comb my hair and drag my feet. I open it to an incredibly uncomfortable looking Gabriel Deluca.

"What do you want?"

He sways from foot to foot, picking at his cuticles. One of the most unbearable things about Gabe is how relatable all of his tells are. He catches me fixing my hair and switches to trying to tame his own dark curls. He doesn't have to though. Unruly hair on guys is hot. Unruly hair on girls—or maybe just on girls that look like me—is just lazy.

"My mom said we should offer you a ride." Gabe mumbles.

He's a chronic mumbler.

"You know, since we live in the same building and everything." He finally straightens, trying to peer past me into the apartment. "Is Marnie..."

"Pretty sure she already left."

He nods once. "Come on then, I guess."

I frown. "Would she not have been invited?"

"My mom only mentioned—"

"Was Marnie not invited?" I repeat.

Gabe just shrugs.

"See you in class." I try to slam the door in his face, but he puts out his foot to stop it.

"Frick!" He hops away. "What the—"

I roll my eyes. "You shouldn't go around sticking your foot in doorways, asshole."

He glares, but when he puts his foot back down, he winces instead of retorting. That's what gives his away.

28

I frown. "You're actually hurt?"

"A bit, yeah. I..." he tries to stand on it again and his face screws back up. "Dammit!"

I look from him back into my apartment. I am running late, but breathing the same air as him already feels like betraying Marnie. I sigh, grabbing my backpack. I can feel him watching me lock the door as he hobbles and waits.

"I'll help you to the elevator," I say. "You're on your own after that."

He nods. "Thank you."

I'm not a fan of touching people I'm not close to. I'm not sure if that's just something that comes along with being me or if it's more the product of inhabiting the kind of body that makes other people hyper aware of every inch of your skin, but I try to avoid touching most people whenever possible.

Not Marnie though. She's the exception to every rule. If she hadn't suddenly lost it, we'd probably be walking to school together hand in hand just because we could. Instead, I have one arm wrapped around the boy I hate's waist, he has one thrown over my shoulder, and we're slowly hobbling our way to the elevator.

The elevator that's apparently out of order.

He turns to look at me.

"No."

"You're the one who—"

"I didn't ask you to shove your foot in the way!"

He's quiet.

"Ask me," I decide. I won't be able to leave him alone, after all. It'd be a bit awkward running into his mother downstairs without him. She'd tell Pia because even though I'm pretty sure Mrs. Deluca's never stepped foot in Italy, they decided that her husband made them kindred spirits the moment that she moved into our building. And Pia would tell my mom or Marnie or someone else awful. If I can't leave him, I can at least rub it in a little.

29

"What?"

"Ask me to help you downstairs. Politely."

Gabe rolls his eyes. "I'll be fine in a bit."

"Probably," I shrug. "You'll also be late."

He sighs. "Please help me downstairs," he mumbles.

I cock my head to the side. "I don't know if that sounded very—"

"Cory!"

"Ask me."

He swallows. Looks straight at me. "I would really appreciate it if you helped me downstairs. Please."

It still feels like pulling teeth, but I don't feel like being late either, so I take it. "Even though you're a homophobic bag of dicks?" I add.

He just glares.

I pull out my phone to check the time. "Bell rings pretty soon. Today's the first day of our B-schedule too, so—"

"Even though you don't like me," he says through gritted teeth.

I frown. "I don't think that's what I said, actually."

"You're an actual toddler."

"Okay," I start towards the stairwell. "See you at school then, I guess."

"Cory!" He calls after me.

I don't turn around.

"Cory!" He repeats. He sighs. "I'm... I'm a big bag of dicks, okay?"

I grin. It isn't exactly on script, but his version's even better.

I skip back over to him, just to rub his nose in my own lack of injury. "Let's go exploit your mom then."

Tragically, Gabe's back to near full mobility by the time his mother drops us off at the end of the parking lot. Neither one of us ask her to drop us closer though, so I hover nearby as he dramatically stumbles his way into the building.

"You can't possibly still be that hurt," I call him out. "It was just a door."

"Maybe you're just freakishly strong!"

"Or you're just freakishly brittle."

I need to find a way to distance myself from him again, but that's difficult when you're headed in the same direction. Someone from elementary school could see us. Someone could get the wrong idea.

I still haven't managed to fully lose him by the time we enter the school and then, we continue in the same direction.

"No," I realize. Instead of having two separate semesters like some of the other high schools in the area, we have the same classes year-round. They just alternate based on the day of the week. I am not about to be stuck having a whole year of morning classes with Gabe Deluca.

"Drama?" He guesses.

I groan. He, annoyingly, smiles.

"Relax. It's probably a big class. You can spend all year hating me from afar."

I freeze. "I have every right to hate you."

He nods once.

"This isn't some petty elementary school... you're an awful person. That isn't something you get to joke about."

"Okay," he pulls open the door to the theatre. It's just more proof that he isn't actually as injured as he's pretending to be. "hate me from afar then."

Nonymous

Chapter 5

Drama class in high school is a completely different experience to drama class in elementary school.

It's a graduation requirement to have at least one arts credit, so all the artistic kids take visual arts, all the smart kids take instrumental music, and then actual theatre kids get lobbed together with the rest of us. A theoretical increase in the proportion of kids that actually like theatre should make it run more smoothly, but without the quiet kids there to balance us out, it's supposed to be pandemonium.

I knew that Marnie would hate it. That's why I told her that we could take something else over and over again when we were first picking our courses last year. And yet, even though she insisted that it would be fine, she's suddenly decided that she had to get rid of both me and the class.

Somehow (despite the fact that both logic and guidance counsellors imply that ninth grade drama classrooms should be full of untalented amateurs) everyone seems to know each other. They whisper and laugh and sing songs that are vaguely familiar in that way that all showtunes are vaguely familiar. They talk about summer camp and after school programs. The teacher Mr. McCoy's name fills the room long before he's arrived. Something about him's summoned all the theatre kids here.

I'm outgoing. Normally. But I've never been outgoing without knowing that Marnie would be right there for me to return to if I got shut down. It's a lot more difficult to be speak up for myself when it's entirely on my own behalf. Gabe's the only person I recognize and seems equally out of place, but every time he starts to gravitate towards me, I manage to glare harshly enough that he gets the hint and wonders off again.

And then, ten full minutes after the bell, he arrives.

Mr. McCoy is just some guy. His hair's part brown part grey and is clearly starting to thin at the top. He's of an average height and an average weight. His eyes are brown. He wears a polo shirt and khakis and is the most 'some guy' guy that's ever existed, but I'm pretty sure half of the class is a single breath away from applauding.

He smiles, says "sorry I'm late" and maybe it's some kind of joke I missed, because the room laughs. There's a circle of chairs in the centre of the theatre, but he sits down in front of one and we all follow suit. He looks around the group before extending a finger towards Gabe.

"Gabriel," he says.

Gabe tries to sink down into his t-shirt and I suddenly decide to give Mr. McCoy a chance.

"I don't know you yet," Mr. McCoy continues.

"Gabe," Gabe corrects, probably realizing that he's supposed to say something.

Every other pair of eyes becomes even more focused on Mr. McCoy than they already were.

Mr. McCoy's laugh is wheezing. "We'll use Gabriel here," he says. "More star potential."

Gabe just blinks.

I know that his finger will attack me next, so when he starts to say, "Corrina," I cut him off.

"It's just Cory."

A few people laugh uncomfortably. Most don't.

He repeats it again, rolling the 'r' this time for emphasis even though he's definitely gotten it off of an attendance sheet and my last name makes it extremely clear that I'm not from any kind of country that would pronounce it that way.

"I prefer Cory, thanks."

He frowns then grins, raising an eyebrow and looking around the circle. "Well then, Gabriel and *Cory*. The rest of us had the privilege of getting to know each other at camp this summer, but you guys can call me Brian. I'm really dedicated to keeping things cool and comfortable here. If anyone wants to try out any new names or pronouns, this is—"

"It's always just been Cory," I stop him again. "She/her, please."

I've decided that I'm back to not liking Mr. McCoy. There are few quicker ways to end up on my hate list than insisting on calling me Corrina.

Mr. McCoy is seemingly some kind of actor, but his smile's still obviously tight. He goes around the circle again to get everyone else's pronouns, leads us through a bunch of awkward theatre games, and ignores me for the rest of the class which suits me just fine.

I piece things together as the class progresses. Mr. McCoy (or Brian, but only ever when he's within earshot) just finished getting his teaching degree after running one of the only two theatre programs in town for years. The pretentious one. The 'extensive' one (that's really just code for 'not fun'). Almost everyone else here catered their schedules specifically to spend more time around him between summers.

We sit back down in front of our chairs again just before the bell. "Curriculum," Mr. McCoy says. "Dictates that I spend months on mime and silent acting to build up your confidence." He pulls a folder far too thin to hold an actual curriculum document within it out of his bag and dramatically tears it in two. "We're going to do things our own way this year."

A few people actually cheer.

Mr. McCoy smiles. "Before next class, everyone needs to pair up! Choose wisely, you'll be working together all year and if you want to do well, it'll require a lot of out of school practicing. You're going to know your partners better than they even know themselves."

The moment he mentions pairs, almost everyone's already taken. Best friends latch hands. Crushes are stared at. All that's left is me, Gabe, and two boys that I don't recognize. I walk up to one as he's packing his bag.

"Partners?"

He looks behind me, clearly waiting for someone else, but then gives in and pretends to smile. "Sure! Swap numbers?"

I hand him my phone then beeline for my next class. Hopefully he's put his name in with his number so I won't have to awkwardly ask what it is.

Gabe jogs after me as I leave the theatre. I walk faster.

"Cory!" He catches up.

"Leg seems better," I mutter.

"Do you have a partner?"

I stop to glare at him more effectively. "You're the last person I'd pair up with."

He sighs. "We'll give you rides. The whole year."

"I didn't even—"

He grabs my arm. "Cory. Please."

I'll savour his pleading later. For now, I have to get to class. "There's an even number. Just pair up with what's his face. The guy with all the freckles. Who doesn't hate you yet."

Gabe fiddles with his hair. "I really don't want to."

I frown. "What could you possibly have against him? I'm the one who..." And I remember. That Gabe's the worst. "Holy crap, Gabe."

He must realize that I've realized, because he has the decency to look guilty.

"Please just—"

"You can't catch being gay, you know. You also can't just tell if someone is. You—"

"I know, okay? Just... please."

"No! You have to—" I finally flip my phone around to figure out the name of the guy that I've promised to partner up with and find a text instead.

Marnie: You walked to school with Gabe?

I swallow. I'm an awful person and I know that even as I consider it, but if being an awful person gets Marnie to keep talking to me, I can deal with that. "Fine," I pretend to relent for his sake. "I'll text my partner and ask to switch. But you owe me forever."

I leave Marnie on read.

Chapter 6

"Gabriel and Corrina," Mr. McCoy claps as soon as he's finished luring us all into his circle Friday morning. He's in a constant state of clapping even though his voice is loud enough to hold our attention all on its own.

"Cory," I correct.

This time, no one laughs.

"Yes," Mr. McCoy pretends to remember. "Of course." He pulls two sheets of paper out of a folder and extends them out towards us. "Since you're our newcomers, why don't the two of you go first?"

"Just... read it?" Gabe checks.

"Of course not!" He grins, gesturing towards the stage. "Act it!"

I take the paper and trudge my way up. Then assume that I'm being pranked.

"Hi," I read my first line.

Gabe takes a while to respond, likely also questioning every decision that's brought him to this point. "Hi."

"Hi," I read again.

And so we go. Back and forth for half a minute, twelve words in total, six each. All of them hi.

Mr. McCoy starts to applaud as we awkwardly make our way back to our seats and everyone else tentatively joins in. "Wonderful?" He smiles. "Next?"

The next pair's only word is 'bye'. Their performance is somehow infinitely better than ours. One of them actually starts crying.

It was a trap, though, I realize as everyone else follows suit. These kids know Mr. McCoy. If he'd sent two of them up first, they would have known to do more than just read their word back and forth at each other. He wanted us to look stupid. I do not like being made to look stupid.

Nonymous

"Okay!" Mr. McCoy claps when we're finally finished. "These," he raises his folder to the air and pauses for dramatic effect. "are your scripts until the end of the year. We'll obviously work on other things too so I don't get in trouble with admin, but every other Friday, we'll go over them again and see what's changed."

He waits for a reaction that none of us give him.

"I can tell some of you think this is silly. Maybe even a waste of your time." I look around the circle and don't know where he's getting that from. If anyone else thinks this is useless, they're certainly not showing it. "But acting begins the moment we're on stage, even if your first line seems inconsequential. Your homework for the weekend," he approaches the whiteboard. "Is to think about first impressions. You and your partner are going to write them on each other. Whether you work collaboratively or not is up to you, but I want you to take this seriously. I'll be sending you prompts to answer later today."

Gabe follows me out of the theatre. I must have done something truly awful over the summer and then forgotten about it, because it seems like Gabe's suddenly following me everywhere.

"When are you free?" He asks.

"What?"

"To answer the questions. When—"

"We don't have to answer them together."

Gabe untucks his hair then pushes it behind his ear again. "I can't let you submit a bunch of unfiltered thoughts about me without looking them over first, Cory."

I cock my head to the side in mock confusion. "Because you're worried I'll mention you're a bigoted asshole?"

He sighs. "Just... when are you free?"

"Never."

"Cor—"

38

"I've gotta go," I speed up. "Guess you'll just have to hope I conveniently forget about the last few years right before I start writing up my answers, huh?"

"Cory, you can't—"

I smile, straighten my backpack strap, and walk into math class.

Gabe does not try to bring it up again on the ride home. It'd be difficult to, with his mother there. It means he won't get another chance to until Monday and by then, it'll already be too late. I won't have to worry about him again all weekend.

And then, footsteps in the hall. Too many footsteps in the hall. I am not above a little peephole spying so I pull over our stepstool (Mom and I are both exceptionally short and exceptionally nosy, so we always make sure it's on hand) and there she is. Marnie out of focus. Marnie with her stomach too long and her head all squished. Marnie and four other girls I don't even recognize chatting and giggling and headed for her apartment where I'm supposed to be on Fridays. In any other universe, I'd be proud of her. I want to be proud of her in this one too, but that hurts a bit too much. I'm outgoing. I'm the extrovert. But Marnie's already made so many friends that I can't even recognize them and I've made absolutely none because every time I've tried to talk to someone all week it's like my throat caves in on itself and I suddenly forget every single word in the English language because every time I try to talk to someone new, all I do is remind myself that I'm no longer talking to her. Maybe I've only ever been able to be outgoing when I knew I'd have Marnie to return to. Maybe I can only be loud on other people's behaves.

I don't slip off the stool. I don't scream or gasp or cry. The hole in my stomach does not extend into the real world and swallow either me or the door whole. But somehow, she still sees me. She stops laughing, for half a second. Her smile goes distant. We make eye contact: me from behind glass and wood and her with her smooshed up face. Then she just shakes her head a bit, grabs the hand of the girl beside her, and pulls her keys out of her pocket.

And then she's gone, just like that. And then she gets to move on, just like that.

I pull out my phone.

Me: *You have fifteen minutes to get up here. After that I'm locking the door and answering the stupid questions myself.*

There's a knock at the door in less than five.

Chapter 7

"Hi."

"Hi."

I don't laugh in the awkward silence that follows after we've accidentally begun reenacting our script because it's somehow even more awkward without the paper there in front of us.

Someone is laughing though. Multiple someones, just down the hall. I flinch and snap back into focus. I step out of the doorway. "I guess you'd better come in then."

Gabe sits down on my couch like he owns the place and starts pulling papers out of his backpack. "You're fighting then," he mumbles. "That... actually makes a lot of sense."

"I'm not—we've been fighting for basically—"

"With Marnie, I mean."

I don't know what to say to that.

"Guess that explains why you kept insisting I meet you up here instead of in the parking garage. And way earlier than you normally leave. You're trying not to look all sad and pathetic."

I scoff. "I'd rather actually be sad and pathetic than have to talk to you."

"You wouldn't though, would you?" As he moves his head to the side, the corner of his lips follows suit. I want to throw another door at him or something just to wipe the half-grin away. "Which means you don't actually have any more leverage than I do here. Actually..." he stops to consider. "You're already stuck with me as a partner so I'm pretty sure if we tallied it up—"

"Shut up."

"That puts me on top, right?"

"I said—"

"So that means I could—"

"Get out of my apartment!"

Finally, Gabe stops smiling. "Cory, I'm just messing with you. No nefarious schemes, I—"

"I could still write all about how much you suck," I remind him. "Being an awful person might not have phased that many teachers in middle school but our hyper-performatively accepting, possibly actually gay drama teacher might take at least a little offense."

He just nods. "We're even then, okay? Mutually assured destruction or... I guess one-sided assured destruction, one sided exploitative partnership or whatever."

I swallow. Gabe knowing that I'm relying on him for something is infinitely more soul crushing than the actual relying on him part was.

"Marnie and I are just taking some space from each other," I admit. "For a bit."

"Sounds messy."

"It's not. We're fine and we're going to be fine so don't... if you try to say a single rude thing about Marnie or her being a lesbian or—"

He raises his arms in surrender. "Understood." Gabe pulls his legs up onto the couch and slides his laptop out of his bag. "Have you looked at the questions yet?"

"No," I admit. I'd been planning on leaving them until Sunday night.

Gabe nods. "I can make a shared google doc, then? I'll write down your answers too so you won't have to bother doing it yourself and then I'll just submit for both of us so it's easier for him to mark."

I narrow my eyes at him. "And so that you can look over my answers."

"Absolutely and so that I can look over your answers. It'll be shared with you too, though, so you can make sure I don't outright lie."

"Fine." I finally let myself sit down. On a completely separate couch. On a completely separate side of that completely separate couch. "What's the first question?"

"Describe your partner physically," he reads.

I blink. "He did not write that."

He flips his laptop around to prove it.

I sigh. This has to be against some kind of standard teacher rule, but Mr. McCoy doesn't seem like the kind of person who cares about those sorts of things.

"Describe your partner physically," Gabe prompts again. "What are the first things you notice about them?"

"You're short," I volunteer.

His eyes go wide. "I'm taller than you!"

"Boy short, then," I shrug.

"I'm—"

"Do you really want to give me time to come up with something else instead?"

Gabe sighs and types. I'm pretty sure he adds in the 'boy' part.

"You're average height then," he decides. "People short for sure, but only a bit under girl average."

"You have acne."

Gabe rolls his eyes. "I thought the point of doing it together was to make sure neither of us comes across as an asshole."

"That wasn't an asshole thing to point out," I defend myself. "Maybe if I didn't also have acne, but it's the kind of thing he'd expect us to notice. Just write it for me too."

He doesn't type.

I sigh. I didn't even mean that one to be particularly insulting, it just felt like the safest option. His appearance has nothing to do with why he sucks so stooping that low intentionally would just mean that I'm kind of an awful person too. Plus, Gabe's annoyingly good looking, for an asshole. His eyes are big and bright and his skin's the perfect shade of bronze to compliment his hair and even there he somehow makes messiness look good. I just can't say any of that without giving him the wrong idea, so acne felt like the most neutral thing to point out. Boys can be so sensitive though.

"You don't have to," I concede. "On either of ours. I would've put it on like, 90% of the class's sheets anyway though, for the record. Everything else about you's annoying enough that I don't have to resort to appearance-based attacks."

"Let's put it on neither," he decides.

"Okay, fine. Whatever. Your hair's dark, curly, and always messy." No more no less. The most negative sounding adjective at the end to make sure that it's the one he remembers. I refuse to boost Gabriel DeLuca's ego.

"Yours is light, curly, and always messy. And long, I guess," he adds.

I nod. "Your eyes are brown." No specific shade.

"Yours are grey."

"Blue," I correct.

"They're definitely not. And these are my first impressions, so I get to decide. We can probably move onto the next—"

"You're thin," I say since he's obviously not man enough to do it first. It's not the kind of thing every single other student is necessarily writing in their first-impression responses, but it is something that they'd all put on mine. "You'd be gangly if you were taller. Not sure if that still works for short people though."

"Okay." He adds it. "Thin, almost gangly. Next question."

I sigh. "Gabe."

"It's—"

"Gabe! You have to write mine too. That obviously counts as something people'd notice about me."

He sucks on his lip, keeping his eyes on the screen. "I'm not... I don't want to come across as offensive."

"Okay, wow."

His ears go red.

"That's somehow way more offensive then literally anything you could have ever written, just for the record."

His ears somehow go redder. He's quiet and they can't type for him though, so I roll my eyes.

44

"I know I'm fat, Gabe. I'm not going to suddenly start questioning my entire existence if you confirm it. And believe it or not, that's definitely something that people tend to notice pretty quickly, so I'm pretty sure you're supposed to write it down."

"Fine. Whatever."

He types. I pull out my phone to check his work.

"Than what?" I ask.

"What?"

"I'm 'heavier' than what?"

Gabe just sighs. "What do I write then?"

"Fat, probably?" I shrug. "Or whatever word actually pops into your head when you look at me? You know, like we're being graded on doing? I know it definitely isn't 'heavier'."

"I tend to go for 'annoying' or 'talks to much' or 'insufferable' first," he mutters.

"Ha."

He deletes *heavier*. He writes *plus-sized*.

I delete *plus-sized*.

"That's also definitely not what you think in your head."

"I can't write fat, Cory. That'd—"

"I called you thin which is literally the exact opposite of fat. They're measuring the same thing so why was that okay and this isn't? I also called you gangly which actually was an insult, by the way."

He sighs. "I don't have any issue with your weight."

"Mmm, it kind of seems like you do."

"Just because—"

"I don't either, for the record, but it's kind of hard to be fine with your body when the rest of the world decides to act like the only appropriate way to talk about it is by pretending that it doesn't exist."

He picks at his cuticle. "You want my real first impressions? Of you physically? What I think in my head where I don't have to filter it for anyone else?"

I shrug. "That's the assignment, right?"

45

"Fine." He leans forward. "You're blonde. You used to be more blonde but that suited you less. Your hair's constantly frizzy and you should probably look into using a better shampoo or something because I'm pretty sure that's not supposed to happen. Writing 'you're shortish' was also technically a lie because I actually think 'you're about half an inch shorter than me' because I measure everyone's height in relation to my own. You're fat, you have freckles right now but they'll go away more in the winter. Your eyes are so obviously grey and I genuinely have no idea how you still don't have that right. You used to be awful at dressing yourself and now you just wear jeans all the time to pretend you're still not. And—and again, this is purely just physical impressions—you'd be kind of pretty. Minus the inability to dress yourself and constant scowling and—"

I accidentally scowl and help prove his point. "That's just around you. I don't constantly—"

"Yeah," he says. "I figured. But they're my first impressions. I get to write all of that or none of that because sure, people shouldn't only describe weight neutrally in one direction, but they do. If I give a bullet list of points and put that on there, I'm going to look like an asshole."

I sigh. "Fine. Whatever. You have my permission to tell Mr. McCoy how pretty you think I am."

"That was one tiny part of it surrounded by a bunch of ifs you didn't even let me finish. There's also your personality and—"

"I'm not adding pretty to yours no matter how much you keep buttering me up."

He rolls his eyes. "Fine, whatever. Next question then," he scrolls. "Recall the first time you met your partner, whether in this class or otherwise. What did you think of them after that first meeting?"

"I thought you were rude," I say instantly. "We were all playing tag waiting for the bell to ring and classes to start and you weren't respecting the sanctity of no tag backs."

"He'll probably want more than just rude," Gabe points out.

"Selfish too then," I supplement. "And a bad listener. Your turn."

"I thought you seemed interesting. Exciting."

I snort. "Liar. I yelled at you so much that multiple adults ran over to pull my away."

He shakes his head. "That was the first day of senior kindergarten. Definitely thought you sucked after that, but the first time I saw you, you were five and trying to slide down the cement rail thing to the bottom of the parking garage and your knees were already all screwed up because you'd clearly been trying for a while, but you kept going anyway. Recklessly endangering your life is like the number one way to make little boys want to be your friends."

I frown. "Doesn't count. We didn't actually meet."

"Well, it makes me sound like a way better person than you, so that's what we're going with. Last question," he scrolls. "What do you think of your partner now?"

I start to answer then stop myself. I realize that I really, really, don't want to hear Gabe's. His opinion is and always has been the last thing I've ever cared about, but he's also one of the only other people who's known me for essentially my entire conscious life. Maybe Marnie has a valid reason for cutting me off that I just haven't found yet. Maybe he'll write something a bit too close to the truth. I am not ready to know that yet. "Let's do that one ourselves," I decide. "More authentic."

He frowns. "Cory..."

"You can still look it over since it'll be on the same document, stupid. I'll lie and be boring anyway. Nothing to worry about."

And I do. I stick to facts: Gabe is in my drama class, Gabe has a better memory than me, Gabe lives on the third floor. Facts are safe. I don't read what he writes and promise myself that I never will.

47

It was a bad idea to suggest that we write on our own though. Because once we start, we stop talking. Once we stop talking, I can hear her. Shrieking and laughing and living with people who aren't me.

"Done?" Gabe checks.

The sudden noise makes me jump. I blink my way back into the room. "What? Yeah."

He sighs. He puts his laptop and papers back away, stands up, and holds out a hand. "Let's go."

"What?"

"No point in me being here if we don't go show her how cool and sociable you are, right? Let's go make her jealous."

Chapter 8

"We're gonna get in trouble."

Gabe rolls his eyes. "You sound like Marnie."

That snaps me into reality. The boy who just helped me set up pillows all the way down the hallway is not just some guy. This is Gabriel DeLuca. This is our sworn enemy.

This is all wrong.

I pick the pillow closest to me back up and he sighs. "Cory."

"Don't pretend you know literally anything about her."

"Okay," he says. "Sorry, whatever. Just leave everything where it is, okay? Give me the lid."

I hug it against my stomach. "This was stupid. We'll get in trouble. It's disruptive."

"That's kind of the whole point. It's not even 4pm yet, I bet barely anyone's home."

"I'm not doing it."

"Fine, be boring." He holds out his hand. "I didn't lug all this up here for nothing though, so let me."

Maybe it'll work in my favour if Gabe and his family get in trouble once enough residence complain about him sliding around on a storage lid in the hall. Maybe they'll get kicked out and he'll change schools and I'll be able to pretend that I did it on purpose for Marnie's sake, so she'll finally remember how obsessed with each other we're supposed to be. For that to work though, I can't be caught at the scene of the crime, so I say "fine," hand him the lid, and walk back into my apartment. I'm not immune to curiosity though. I pull the stool back over and do my best to watch through the peephole.

Storage Bin Obstacle Course had been Gabe's idea, but he's somehow still awful at it. He stands and kicks and sits and pushes and lies down and pulls and never even makes it to the first pillow. It's so pathetic that standing by and watching somehow feels more illegal than participating. I open the door again and hold out a hand. "Give it."

"I don't think it's working."

"Give it."

Gabe relents, handing over the lid.

I hold it against my chest, give myself a bit of space to run into it, then fall onto my stomach and make it a few feet before crashing into a pillow and losing my momentum.

I grin in triumph, walking back to him to hand over the lid. "See? That's how it's done."

"You hit the first obstacle."

"I... you couldn't even get yourself going!"

He just shrugs.

"Give it back."

"No," he laughs. "It's my turn!"

"You already had a ton of turns. Give it back."

"Fine." He starts to hand it over then jumps to the side, miserably miscalculating his own momentum and landing with a loud thud.

I cackle and pull out the lid from where it's lodged itself under his knee.

"That one didn't count," he mumbles.

"Oh, it absolutely did."

My second try, I manage to maneuver around the first two pillows by pushing my legs against the walls. By the third, I make it halfway down the course. Once we've both gotten it down and there's nothing left for me to gloat over, I begin timing it.

We're loud. We're so loud that they must hear us down on the floor below us and maybe I should be worried about that, but my voice of reason decided that we needed to take a break from each other. We're loud and ridiculous and probably breaking at least two tenancy rules, but I'm having fun, so I decide I don't care. It's nice, not having to care.

That doesn't mean that it's nice not being with Marnie. That definitely doesn't mean that it's nice being with Gabe. But maybe once she comes to her senses and things go back to normal, we can try to be a little more carefree.

I've almost beaten my record when a door at the end of the hall slams open. "What the—"

I roll off the tray, letting it skid into the wall. Before I'm even on my feet, Gabe's hands are on my arm, pulling me back towards my apartment.

We slam the door shut behind us. We haven't run more than a few steps, but adrenaline must be making his blood pump too, because we both collapse against the wall, catching our breaths.

"That was—" Gabe starts.

"Shh!"

We wait longer.

"I'm pretty sure—"

"Shh!" I urge again.

He nods, but I already know that it's coming. He bites down on his lip. His shoulders start to shake. Then, all at once, he bursts into laughter.

"Shush!" I lunge at him to cover his mouth and at least succeed at knocking him into the welcome mat, but it's too late. I've already heard it. There's nothing left to stop me from laughing too.

"Oh my god!" I manage once I've finally caught my breath. Again. There's no point in being quiet now anyway. "That was... do you think they'll know it was us?"

"There are cameras in the hall, Cory. If anyone complains, it wouldn't be hard to figure it out."

I punch his arm. "Why didn't you mention that earlier!"

"I wanted to have fun," he shrugs. He sighs when he realizes that I'm no longer smiling. "It'll be fine. I've been doing stupid crap all summer. My parents'll send someone a fruit basket and a note about unruly teenagers or something if they complain."

"This was so—"

"Shh," Gabe stops me this time. "Listen."

For some reason, I do. "I hear... nothing?"

"Exactly. Did you notice that? While we were in the hall? Her apartment sudden went completely silent. They definitely noticed. Mission accomplished." He holds out an arm for a fist bump and something about it (or maybe something about him bringing up Marnie) forces me to remember who he is.

I'd been having fun. I'd been having fun with Gabriel DeLuca.

I stand up and smooth out my jeans. "You should probably go then. We finished everything we had to."

He frowns. "Wait, what did I—"

"We're not friends, Gabe. I don't even like you."

He rolls his eyes. "Right, well last time I checked you didn't have anyone else lined up to talk to and I'm frankly terrified of actual drama kids and don't know anyone else our age in the building, so if you ever get over yourself and—"

"I won't."

"Fine." He gets up. "Enjoy being lonely and bitter then, I guess. See you next time one of us needs the other for something."

"See you in drama."

Chapter 8

On Monday, we read our reports on each other out loud. Luckily, Mr. McCoy has the subject of each presentation leave the room while their partner presents for "authenticity", so I at least don't have to listen to Gabe talking about me.

When it's my turn to present my answers to the final question, Mr. McCoy never stops frowning.

"Tell me more," he says.

"That's all I wrote."

He shakes his head. "Tell me more. Tell me anything."

"His parents are—"

The head shaking doesn't stop. "You're telling me about a mannequin, Corrina. Make him into a person."

The problem isn't that I don't know enough about Gabe to do that. I've spent a lifetime learning far too much about Gabriel Deluca, actually.

I've already said that he moved to our apartment building when we were all five, but I didn't mention how much I'd hated that. I didn't explain that he was the third kid our age (maybe not in the entire building, but in the parts that we knew about) and that Pia (who's eternally nostalgic for the country she's too anxious and busy to return to) took one look at his father when she caught them walking home from school one day and decided that not only should he also start playing with us, but that she liked him more than me. I could say that he was my first rival because even though she didn't say it outright, I could tell.

"Don't they make such a cute little couple?" When there were three of us in a room together.

"Awww, look how sweet they are with each other!" when I'd been holding Marnie's hand moments before.

I don't think I was old enough to process that they were talking about crushes and weird little heteronormative baby weddings and I definitely wasn't old enough to process liking boys

53

or girls or anything beyond sugar, but maybe that's why it made me so mad.

That Marnie didn't even like him all that much outside of apartment building playdates and that I was the one who she'd swap stickers and friendship bracelets with and bother teachers about sitting beside, but Gabe's existence somehow made the adults in our lives decide that I was less important to her than he was.

I could tell them that I kept going to their stupid building get togethers even as we all got older and they became less frequent as it stopped being deniable that while Marnie and I were just as obsessed with each other as our moms were with themselves, Gabe never clicked with either of us the way in the way that his parents did with ours. That I kept going because I didn't particularly like having to hang out with him, but I definitely wasn't going to let him hang out alone with Marnie because no matter how much evidence I collected to the contrary, I was always at least a bit afraid that he'd randomly swoop in one day and take her away from me.

I could list all his favourite desserts and games and TV shows growing up. How many bones he's broken, where, and how. I could describe the sound of his laugh because I've accidentally memorized it over the year (it's incredibly grating), the sound of his tears because he was a massive cry baby when we were little, and even the noise he makes when he sneezes.

I could also say that Marnie never disliked him, so I tried my very best not to either as we got older. That at some point I was able to start recognizing that I was jealous over nothing. That when she realized that she was a lesbian in sixth grade she told me, then we told the moms together, then she told him (almost accidentally. His mom made a stupid comment about the babies they'd make one day and she corrected her), and then she was suddenly telling the entire school because he couldn't keep his freaking mouth shut for one second. I could say that Marnie would have forgiven him if he'd apologized or said that it had been a mistake and that he'd definitely known that Marnie would have forgiven him if he'd apologized or said that it had been a mistake but instead, he doubled down and ring-led a few weeks of stupid homophobic jokes and then kept it going for the rest of the school year even after everyone else had gotten bored and moved on. That he kept it going even when I threatened him and that he kept it going even when he caught Marnie crying and that he kept it going even after I stopped threatening him and punched him in his stupid little homophobic face and that then, at least, the meetings ending because our parents had to get involved and that eventually (painfully slowly) he stopped talking about Marnie at all.

I could also say that he started the student tutoring program in middle school that I refused to go no matter how many teachers referred me out of spite. I could say he volunteers at camps in the summers and referees little kid soccer games for free on the weekends sometimes. I could say that by all accounts, in all areas beyond one of the most important ones, Gabriel DeLuca is an upstanding member of our community.

The problem has never been that I don't know enough about Gabe to make him a person. The real problem's that I know too much. There is no possible way to shove all the pieces of him that I've collected over the years together to make someone who feels real. Everyone's better off if I never try to assemble him at all. I need to keep him as a jumble of disassembled pieces because I know exactly which one doesn't fit and I can never let myself pretend that that one doesn't exist.

So, I pretend to think about it and say, "he's half Italian."

"More," Mr. McCoy urges.

"On his dad's side."

"More! There must be—"

I look him straight in the eye. "His mum's parents are English, I think."

Nonymous

I'm peppered with questions from my classmates before Gabe's invited back into the room, and I answer, "I don't know," to each and every one of them.

Chapter 9

When I open my door that Friday to get our next weekend's worth of drama homework out of the way, Gabe has his hands shoved into his pockets.

"Okay, don't hate me, okay? This'll be a lot more annoying if—"

I roll my eyes. "A little late for that. Come in. Let's get this over with."

He frowns. "Did you not see it yet?"

"What?"

He pulls out the phone. "Last week's work. He marked it as incomplete."

I really, really, hate theatre people.

"I'm..." I pause, realizing that Gabe clearly thinks that this is somehow his fault. "Wait, what did you do?"

He blushes. "Maybe I didn't answer all of his follow up questions?"

"Oh." Normally I'd be mad about someone sabotaging an assignment, but this means I won't have to admit to doing the exact same thing.

"He kept trying to correct me on name stuff which, okay, hindsight, probably should have just let him because then all his follow up questions were about gender and sexuality and—"

"That can't possibly be allowed."

"Right? He's insane."

I bristle, realizing that we likely think it's inappropriate for entirely different reasons.

"Anyway, I felt uncomfortable feeding into that so I just kind of refused to and he seemed pissed. Sorry. Next time—"

"I'd rather you still don't talk about my sexuality with our teacher next time."

"Right," he scratches at his elbow. "Yeah. Good call."

57

I sit down on the couch and wait for him to follow. I don't tell him that Mr. McCoy's also mad at me. If he wants all the blame, he can keep it.

"Anyway," I start to power on my computer. "We should—"

"I'd be fine with you being... whatever you end up being. For the record," he says.

I roll my eyes. "Liar."

"I'm not... seriously, it'd be fine. Obviously whether or not I think it's fine wouldn't impact—"

"I'm straight. Whether or not I like the stereotypically more feminine or masculine form of my name has nothing to do with any of that."

He nods. "Okay, cool." Gabe's eyes widen. "Not that it wouldn't also be cool if—"

"Stop it. I'm already obviously fine with working with you. I'd rather you didn't lie to my face to try and get on my good side."

"I'm not doing that!"

I turn my attention back to the computer. No point arguing with a wall. "Question one: what's your partner's favorite childhood memory?"

"Cory, we were—"

"I don't want to spend forever on this, I have other work to do too. Favourite memory, go."

He sighs. "It's camp. I'm nine. We're doing this rope course thing where you have to pull yourself across to the other side and I'm absolutely horrific at it. Poor grip strength. It's my first time at a gender segregated camp so I'm trying for the sixth time all panicked and hot because I guess I figured guys would be more competitive at sports stuff and not only was I letting down my entire team, but everyone else had already finished a few attempts ago so we already knew we were in last. But instead, everyone—even the guys who weren't on my team—crowd around and start cheering me on and a few climb on each other's shoulders to tug at the rope and make it more taunt so I could finally get across and when I do, they erupt into applause and hold me up against the sky and I guess... saying that back it sounds patronizing and embarrassing but somehow it wasn't, you know?"

I frown. "That's a lot of words. I'm going with 'when he finally finished the rope course at camp'. I'll just add more when he inevitably prompts me about it."

"Fine. Whatever. What's yours?"

I suck on my lip. It feels extra wrong talking about her with him, but of course it's Marnie. All of my good memories are full of Marnie. "We were in fifth grade. It was our first big kid school dance, whatever that means. Marn hates dances, especially the middle school ones that are more screaming and jumping than actual music which worked out perfectly for me because I'm an awful dancer. She snuck off to the bathroom so I snuck off to the bathroom and then we found an empty classroom to hide out in and we weren't doing anything actually all that scandalous—we literally just took 'Scrabble' off a shelf and played that for the rest of the two hours—but you could still hear the music in the background and we were too nervous to turn on any lights so we had to play right beside the window and go completely silent anytime we heard anyone walk by and it was probably the most thrilled I've ever felt."

"I'll go with 'ditch a school dance with a friend', then."

I feel my cheeks go warm. I know I've said far too much, but maybe that's a side effect of Marnie withdrawal. I click down to the next question.

"Worst childhood memory."

He shrugs. "You already know."

"No, I don't."

Gabe sighs. "As far as I know, I've only done one majorly asshole-ish thing worth regretting."

"A series of related compounding asshole-ish things," I correct.

"Fine, whatever. That, obviously." He fiddles with his hair. "Could you... if you guys ever end up talking again—"

"When."

"Sure, when. Just... tell her I'm sorry, okay?"

I squint at him. "You're not," I decide.

He sighs. "Cory, I was a kid."

"It was only a few years ago."

"It was a mistake. Not everyone's wildly informed on queer issues in middle school."

"You didn't have to be informed! Maybe you can blame that on not getting that it was a secret, but you were awful to her after! You don't get to pretend treating people with basic freaking kindness requires having a degree in queer theory."

He winces. "Fine, you're right. I'm just... I'm sorry, okay?"

I shake my head. "Tell her that yourself."

"I can't."

I knew that already. Because he's not being serious. He's trying to get me to write that down so that if I ever do decide to expose him to the class, he'll get to play the misinformed, overly apologetic asshole. I will not help him frame hurting her as a mistake. "She liked you, you know" I say. "As a friend. I could never understand why but—"

"Yeah," he stops me. "I know."

"I'm not writing that down."

"That's my answer."

I shrug. "Give me a new one."

"Cory."

"Gabe."

He sighs. "I don't know. Probably just like, hearing my parents fight or something, then."

I nod. That's much more acceptable. "Same, then."

He frowns. "I though you didn't—"

"Same."

He types it out.

60

"Third question's just 'what does this all tell you about them?'" I realize. "We don't have to be in the same room to do that one."

I get up and open the door.

"See you Monday," he says.

I just shrug.

I've barely even sat back down when there's a knock at the door less than a minute later. I have no idea what he could have possibly left. I open it ready to yell at him about wasting my time but instead I find Marnie.

"Hi," she says.

Chapter 10

My plan was to be mad. I'd let her come back obviously (obviously), but I'd make her work for it a little first. I'm owed being mad.

Her fists are hidden inside her sweater sleeves and I can see her tugging on the fabric. She's swaying from foot to foot and there's a glossy sheen to her eyes, but they refuse to meet mine, focusing on the carpet instead.

I know what Marnie looks like when she's nervous. I've memorized it. But it's never supposed to happen around me.

"What—"

"I know this isn't fair," she accidentally interrupts. "I know I can't just talk to you whenever I want to talk to you and not... I know this isn't fair, but I need to—"

I step to the side. "Come in."

She hesitates. "I don't think I should—"

"Marnie," I brush my fingertips against the part of her sleeve where a hand should be. "It's fine. Come in."

She sits in the middle of the couch. Her heels point up towards the air and her butt's on the very edge of the cushion. Marnie's always worn her fight or flight obviously. It's supposed to make it easier for me to help her.

I sit down beside her because I'm always supposed to sit down beside her and it was stupid of her to pretend that that wasn't how we worked last time. "Are you okay?" I check.

She nods.

"Did something happen? Did your girlfriend—"

"We're fine. She's great."

I'm an awful person for being a little crushed by that.

"I shouldn't have come," she says again. "I'm... this doesn't mean I'm ready to..."

"Okay," I nod. "That's fine." It's not, but it feels a lot more fine than having to wait longer to find out why she's crying on my couch.

She finally looks at me. "Do you hate me? I didn't want... I wasn't trying to make you hate me."

I roll my eyes. "Don't be stupid. I could never."

"I didn't mean to make it sound like you couldn't," she rambles. "I know I don't get to cut you off then get upset when you don't react the way I—"

"Marnie," I press my knee against hers. "It's... not fine. We're not fine, I don't think. But I'm never going to hate you. If something happened and you need—"

"Why are you hanging out with him?"

I freeze. This is exactly why I was hanging out with him. This is supposed to be exactly what I wanted. But my favourite person in the universe is crying because of me and I suddenly realize that I'm the world's biggest moron.

"Obviously I can't say we have to stop hanging out then get mad over who you choose to talk to instead but we—"

"I still can't stand him Marn, okay?" I squeeze her hand. "You know that. I couldn't stand him even before we knew he was an asshole."

"Then why is he always over!"

I sigh. "We're project partners. It wasn't up to me," I half lie. "Our drama teacher's a real weirdo so I'm probably going to have to keep meeting up with him, but I promise I give him like, so much shit, okay? And his mom offered to drive me to school so that's why he's been... we can start meeting up at his place. If that's easier."

She chews at her lip. "I shouldn't get to tell you—"

"We're going to start meeting up at his place."

She leans against me. "I love you," she whispers. "I miss you."

I gulp down a golf ball. "Yeah, I know. You too."

"I didn't mean to ... you were always so much more outgoing, Cory. And cool and awesome so I figured we'd both get our own awesome friend groups then at the end of the semester we'd have double the friends and... I wasn't trying to leave you all alone. If you need people to hang out with, my friends are—"

I bristle. My shoulder accidentally jostles her jaw and she pulls away. "I have friends."

I don't, but she wasn't supposed to know that. I'm fine with it. I thought it would make it easier when we became friends again.

"Right, sorry," she lies. I hate that she's noticed. I wonder if anyone else has. I don't need other people though. It's always been just me and her and it'll go back to being just me and her. That's how we work. "But if you need... I was being stupid. With the not talking thing. Obviously I want to keep talking. If you—"

"It was a good idea," even as I hear myself say the words, I wish I could swallow them back down. I have no idea what I'm doing. She's handing my exactly what I want.

But if I let her, I'll have to know that we're only friends again because she decided to take pity on me. If I let her, I'll have to live the rest of our lives knowing that we might only be friends because she pities me.

"It's been nice," I lie. "Getting to figure out who I am on my own. It was a good idea."

"Oh," she says. "right."

"I think we should keep keeping our distance," I say. "For now."

She frowns. "You're sure? Because if—"

I laugh. I take a deep breath in to try and relieve the pressure just behind my eyes. "Jeez, Marnie. It's not like I've spent the last couple of weeks suffering. I'd like to think we were never that codependent. It'll be fun. Like an experiment."

She hesitates, but nods. Marnie doesn't know my tells when I'm lying because normally, I never have to lie to her. "Okay then," she stands up. "Right. I'd better umm... let me know, okay? If you change your mind."

I smile and get up to close the door behind her. "See you next semester!" I call as she returns to her apartment.

Nonymous

I shut the door, lock it, and fall onto the couch. I have just over twenty minutes before Mom gets home so if I'm going to cry, it'll have to be quick.

Chapter 11

"So I have to stop picking you up at your apartment because Marnie might see me?"

It's not a question, he's just being willfully dense. I continue pulling Gabe down the stairs.

"Yes." I could have texted him to say that we'd just have to start meeting in the parking garage because I definitely wasn't giving up the extra fifteen minutes of sleep I get to squeeze in now that I have a ride to school every morning, but acknowledging that his contact's in my phone felt too close to acknowledging that he's a person. So, on Monday, I have to work quickly to redirect him.

"Even though the only reason you made me do that in the first place was because Marnie was supposed to see me?"

"Yes," I huff. If someone doesn't fix the elevator soon, I'll figure out how to do it myself.

"You do get that this all seems completely nonsensical, right?"

I blow a strand of hair out of my face. "Marnie doesn't like seeing you around."

"Right," he says slowly. "Which, again, was exactly the point."

I spin around to face him head on the moment we reach the bottom of the stairs. "Look, if it's bothering you that much, I still have enough time to walk, okay? I never really needed rides."

He rolls his eyes. "No need to get all dramatic, I was just asking a question."

"Well, stop asking. We'll have to start working in your apartment too. I told her we'd switch."

He frowns. "My parents get home earlier."

"I know. Your mom's my ride most days. I'm sure they won't object to us working on an actual mandatory assignment."

"I'm not sure if—"

Mrs. DeLuca honks her horn.

"See? I'll ask her myself."

He grabs at my arm. "Cory, you—"

I'm already pulling open the door though, so he lets go.

"Hey Mrs. DeLuca!" I smile. "Gabe and I'll probably have drama homework later this week. Mind if I hang out at yours to get it done at some point?"

She says it's not a problem because of course it's not and that's that. Gabe tries to tail me once we reach the school again, but I ditch him. I'm on a mission. I'm going to make friends.

I am not the kind of person who needs people. Most people. Sometimes when Mom and I go to visit Europe in the summers I hang out with the cousins, but I'm just as happy when we get our own hotel a little ways away and I can choose to be by myself for the two months. I also like to think that I'm not the kind of person who needs to be seen with people. If I was, I would've tried finding other people to hang out with the moment Marnie dropped me. But Marnie is the kind of person who needs people, apparently. So, if I don't find any, in her eyes, I'll become the kind of person who needs help.

So, for a whole week, I try. I bounce from lunch table to lunch table, asking 'this seat taken?' and then trying my best to join into whatever conversation's happening. I am not the kind of person who's afraid of people, but I'm also not the kind of person used to pretending to be someone I'm not. That can make feigning interest in conversations I'm not a part of a bit difficult. So, I pick a new table and then another, but none of it feels quite right. It's only been a couple of weeks, but maybe every friend group's too cemented to be infiltrated.

I talk to seat partners and offer my number so we can share notes if we ever have to, but then the moment the bell rings, they find someone else to talk to. I smile and make a point of introducing myself to every new person I talk to, but none of it sticks.

It's like something's switched in a matter of months. Obviously I knew that making friends in high school wasn't going to be the same as making friends for the first time in elementary. It's been over a decade since I started somewhere new. But last year when our eighth-grade class was paired up with another school from another city on our grad trip, hadn't I made a ton of friends? I have their numbers still, in my phone. No one reached out once the trip had ended, but I'd still managed to convince enough people to like me to trust me with their phone numbers.

And that had been me too. Not Marnie. Not Marnie-and-Cory. We were a package deal, but it was always my job to do the talking first. I've never needed her to make friends before.

So, maybe the change is me. Maybe I've forgotten how to do it. I should have asked her why on Friday. I should have demanded to know what about me she'd notice that she'd wanted to run from so I'd know how to hide it from everyone else.

I could text her. She would tell me.

But even though I'm the one who said we don't have to be close right now, I still need us to be eventually.

And I'm a little terrified that once she says it, once she reveals my biggest faults and lets it hang there where we can both see it, I'll never be able to put it back away ever again.

Chapter 12

I check my phone for the hundred-somethingth time in five minutes. At this rate, it'll die before she gets here.

"She text you yet?"

"Nope."

I don't know why Gabe's not more nervous. If it was my mom, I'd probably wait fifteen minutes, call her once or twice, then give up and walk home. Mrs. DeLuca is freakishly punctual though. She's normally early.

I tap my foot against the pavement and wait. Another five minutes. Another percent gone.

I sigh. "Wanna call her or something?"

He shakes his head. "She never has her ringer on."

"Guess we're walking then. Make sure you let her know not to come get us just in case she's just running late."

I start to walk. He doesn't.

"Gabe." I prompt. "Apartment to reach? Questions to answer?"

"Why don't we just do them here?" He suggests.

"Because then I'll have to spend even more time with you? Come on, we can probably get a lot of it done on the walk there anyway."

"I was planning on stopping by the grocery store before going home. Let's just do it here then split up. I don't want to have to go all the way there and back."

I frown. I hold out a hand. "Give me your phone."

"What?"

"Phone, give it."

He rolls his eyes. "I'm definitely not doing that. You'll throw it into oncoming traffic."

"Gabriel De—"

"Corrina Murphy."

I glare. "Was your mom ever actually coming?"

"What? Yeah. Told you. She's probably late."

69

"And yet you were planning on stopping at the grocery store somehow?"

His ears go red.

I sigh. "Geez, Gabe! What do you have against me going to your place? I already know where you live, it's not like—"

"I just don't think we should work on it there," he mumbles.

"We're not doing it at mine."

"Okay, whatever. We'll—"

"Nope. You're getting over whatever this is because we're apparently stuck doing this for the rest of the year and I'm not gonna freeze my butt off in winter just because—"

"I don't want my parents knowing Mr. McCoy's kind of weird, okay? They'll think the asking students to report on each other's lives thing is creepy and make a big deal out of it."

I shrug. "Maybe they should. I'd be incredibly down to stop."

"They'll make it like a—" he drops his voice. "a gay thing."

I blink. "Did you just... gay's not a slur."

Gabe blushes again. "Yeah, yeah, I know. I—"

"Say it louder."

"What?"

I cross my arms. "If you know, say it louder."

He frowns. "I'm not doing that."

"Fine, whatever. Coward." I sigh. "Do you really need to go to the grocery store?"

He blushes again. "Not really."

"We're going to Tim's instead then so we can actually sit down. You're buying."

I walk off and wait for him to follow.

"I know having homophobic parents doesn't make what I did any more okay," he says.

I slow down a bit, surprised he's said it before I did. I don't want him to notice though, so I pick my speed back up. "Yeah, whatever. Good. It doesn't."

70

"I'm... that's why I didn't want you to know. I didn't want it to seem like... I messed up. Big time. I didn't want it to seem like I was trying to excuse it because I know it was inexcusable."

If he had blamed it on his parents, I would have hated him even more. I'd been expecting him to blame it on his parents.

I don't know what it means now that he isn't. Maybe that he's genuinely meant it every time he's said that he's sorry. Maybe that he genuinely means it when he tries to claim that he's changed. That feels too close to human though, so I push the thought aside. I'm surprised to find that a part of me (too big of a part of me) doesn't want to. A part of me (too big of a part of me) wants Gabriel DeLuca to be redeemable. Maybe I'm not as okay with not having any friends right now as I've been pretending to be.

We get Timbits and hot chocolate. I power on my computer while he pays.

"Where does your partner see themselves in ten years?" I ask once Gabe returns. I pull the box of Timbits closer to myself and fish out a chocolate one.

"Umm..." he considers. "I don't know, really? I guess university would be done by then unless we go for bigger degrees? Married, maybe? Wait, shoot. No, that feels too young to be married. I don't know."

I frown. "I'm supposed to write 'he doesn't know'? Feel like that's just asking for an incomplete again."

He sighs, dipping a Timbit into his hot chocolate. "I'll think of something. You answer first."

"I'll do uni, something businessy, probably. But not to like, start my own company or become uber rich, just for the sake of having something on my resume. I want an office job."

Gabe snorts.

"What! I do!"

"No one dreams of office jobs, Cory."

"Neither do I, that's why it's the perfect job for me."

He just stares so I sigh and explain.

"It's like... maybe not easy, but routine, right? Eventually you can probably turn your brain a bit of the way off and you have a built-in group of people to choose whether or not you want to socialize with every day and a lot of them pay decently enough. If I love something I'd never be able to do it as a job. Every time I try to get serious about a hobby, I end up hating it."

"I think I'd have to do something I love."

I shrug. "That's just you then. Next question: what do you see your partner doing in ten years, try not to default to copying their answer."

Gabe thinks about it. "Office job."

"He said—"

"Not done. Office job but you'd have to be at least in charge of someone because you're crap at authority. And then you'd keep moving up and up even though you'd pretend you don't want to because you'd secretly care about it way more than you'd tell everyone you do because you're weirdly competitive about things."

I smile despite myself. I am known by this boy. I don't want to be this known by this boy. "Decided what you want to be yet?"

He shakes his head.

"Cool. It's incredibly obviously teacher. Or something teaching or childcare adjacent. You might not teach little kids though, I could see you doing high school too. High school or pre-school, the in-betweens wouldn't suit you."

He shrugs. "Yeah, maybe. Better than going with nothing again, I guess."

"And like, one kid and a dog by then, one either on the way or coming soon. Very white picket and boring."

"I can't imagine you marrying anyone," he admits.

I kick him under the table.

"I meant, not as like a 'no one would want to marry you' thing, more that I just don't know your type? Your type was everything breathing in middle school."

I frown. "If this is you trying to ask if I like girls again—"
"It's not. You already said you didn't."
I realize. "You were worried that the two guys were gay."
"What?"
"The two... the only other people left in drama class when we had to pair up. That's why you couldn't partner with them. You thought they were gay."

He blushes. "I thought they might have been and if they weren't, I knew my parents might read any loud theatre boys that way not matter what so yeah, having either of them over wouldn't have been ideal. Not like I would have tried pairing up with you if I had literally any other options."

I wouldn't have paired up with him either. I'd intentionally tried not to until I'd realized that I could use it to try and manipulate Marnie. But at some point I must have forgotten that because for some reason, that hurts. I don't like Gabriel Deluca. I don't actually hate him (not really), but I still also don't like him. I guess some part of me had noticed all the ways he'd been inserting himself into my life all month and wanted it to mean something because it feels good to have people want to be around you.

Gabe notices I'm quiet and frowns. "It's not... I was worried they'd say something stupid or demand I get Mr. McCoy to change my partner. Not that... I don't have anything against it. Not that I even know for sure that either of them are... gay."

I frown. "You did it again."
"What?"
"The whispering thing."
He sighs. "Cory, some people aren't as comfortable with that stuff. I'm trying here."
"Louder."
He rolls his eyes. At just over a whisper, he repeats, "gay."
I shake my head. "Louder."
"You're being ridiculous."
"No, you are. If you're fine with it, why can't you say it?"

"I'm not yelling out gay in a freaking McDonald's."

I stare at him. I start to stand up. He catches on to what's about to happen and tries to pull me down but he's too slow.

"Gay!" I announce. The place is too busy for many people to notice anyway. There's an elementary school nearby so you can't hear much over the sound of children screaming as their parents wait in line for coffee and donuts.

"Cory," Gabe hisses.

"Gay, gay, gay, gay, gay, gay, gay."

"Cor—"

"Gay!" I throw my arms out, wait a second, and sit back down grinning. Gabe's head's still whipping around in alarm, but the few people who did notice are already returning their attention to their food.

I laugh.

"You can't just do that," Gabe whispers. His knee's bouncing so quickly that it hits the underside of the table. I pick up my hot chocolate before he can spill it.

"I thought you said it didn't make you uncomfortable."

"It... you don't just yell stuff like that in public! You can't randomly—"

"Why because it'll make people uncomfortable?"

He's still too busy scanning the restaurant.

"Gabe." I wait for him to look at me. "Promise no one's about to kick us out. But you know what actually might make people uncomfortable? Freaking outing them to an entire school. Or reassuring them that it's 'super okay' to come out to you and very obviously looking for a specific answer. Or just skipping straight to assigning everyone else's sexualities and deciding you're the only straight guy in—"

His shoulders go tight. Normally I wouldn't notice something that small, but that's what Marnie does when she's nervous so I've trained myself to watch for it.

"Oh," I say.

He stands. His knees hit the table on his way up. "We're done the questions now, right? I'm gonna head home."

"Wait, I didn't—"

He picks up his hot chocolate. "You can finish the Timbits."

"Gabe."

He smiles but it's tense and awkward and I don't know how things suddenly flipped and I started feeling like the asshole, but I want to go back to before. "See you Monday."

He leaves.

By the time I pack up all of my stuff (and his since he was in such a rush to get away that he left his entire backpack) and try to follow, I can't find him.

Chapter 13

I break my 'Gabriel DeLuca can't count as a person' rule and text him.

> ***me:*** *where r u*
> ***me:*** *gabe*
> ***me:*** *GABBBEEEEE*
> ***me:*** *i know where you live*

That finally gets me a response.

> ***asshole:*** *I don't want to talk*
> ***asshole:*** *We finished the questions already anyway*
> ***me:*** *i have your backpack, stupid*

He doesn't want to meet at our building, so I follow his directions to a field a few streets away. I find him sitting on top of a hill.

"Hey," I chuck his bag to the ground when I reach him. "Try to be a bit less dysfunctional next time."

He's the one who said he didn't want to talk about it, but then he goes, "whatever you think you've figured out... you didn't."

"Okay," I pretend to believe him. I want to believe him. Every time I learn something new about Gabe he starts to feel just a little bit more like a person and I need to stop that from happening.

He turns to look at me. "I'm serious, Cory."

"Yeah, sure. Whatever. I didn't figure anything out. See you Monday morning."

His shoulders are already starting to shake before I've even finished turning around, but I still go anyway because he doesn't want to talk and I don't want to listen. And he's Gabriel DeLuca.

I almost make it halfway down the hill.

"You were supposed to be gone by now," he mutters, turning away to wipe at his face when I sit down beside him.

"Yeah, well, sucks to suck." I take off my bag and lean against it. "I'm sorry," I make myself admit. "About what I did in Tim's. You were right, that was stupid."

"Most of what you do is."

I'm feeling so guilty that I don't even retort or attack him for that. "I was... maybe I kind of have exactly zero friends right now and was kind of pissed that you were using me even more than I thought you'd been? Not that I want us to be friends, obviously. You're the worst. But I still didn't mean to... that was a big bag of dicks move. Multiple bags."

That earns me a single snort and an eyeroll.

"Obviously you could be queer-positive or queer-neutral or whatever and still not want to scream about it in public."

"I like girls," he says.

"Okay."

"You can't tell anyone."

"That you like girls? I'm sure they'd be—"

"Cory," he stares right at me. His eyes are brown, but they're different than Marnie's. More chestnut than honey. "Seriously."

I swallow. "I know."

"I know it might seem like..." his breathing picks up. "I get I did it to her and it might seem like the perfect way to get back at me, but I—"

"I don't out people," I stop him. "Not even assholes. That'd make me a hypocrite."

His shoulders relax a fraction. "Thank you."

I nod. Saying you're welcome to Gabe would feel too strange. "Guys and girls then?"

"Yeah," he tugs at a hangnail. "I... yeah. I think so. I've been pretty sure for umm... a while now. Since I was like ten."

I could say "me too". It should be easier for me to come out. But I can't make my lips form the words.

"I know that still doesn't make it okay," he fills my silence. "What I did to Marnie. It probably makes it extra bad, honestly. But my parents were freaking out after they heard and until then I hadn't realized... I was mad and scared and confused and I regret it. I wish I'd realized that I'd regret it earlier and she deserves to know that I regret it, but I don't know how to say that without also explaining why I hyperfixated on—" he freezes. "You can't tell her either. You can't—"

"We're not even talking right now, remember?"

"When you do though, you can't—"

"Okay," I nod. "If anyone else finds out, it won't be because of me. I typically try to avoid remembering you exist whenever you're not physically in the room anyway."

"Thank you," he says again.

I look away to save myself from responding. "You still suck. Being gay—"

"Bi."

"Being bi doesn't give you a blanket excuse for sucking."

"Yeah, I know."

"Does anyone else know?"

I'm waiting for him to say yes. I'm not even sure if I'm religious, but I'm practically praying for him to say yes. "Minus like... one boy I kissed at camp four years ago then never talked to again? Nope. No one was ever going to."

I groan. "I guess you can talk about it with me then," I offer. "If you have to."

He rolls his eyes. "Careful. I might start thinking you actually tolerate me."

I push myself back to my feet. He does the same.

"See you Monday?" He says.

I need him to be far from me so I can stop having to feel things more complicated than annoyance. He's gone and had the audacity to accidentally cry a bit in front of me, and now I'm stuck seeing him in 3D again.

He doesn't wait for a response before trying to pass me, so I grab his arm. "Your parents don't know?"

Gabe rolls his eyes. "Obviously not."

"Would they... are you going to be safe? If they find out?"

He tugs at his backpack strap. "I'm... I don't know. Hopefully? Current plan is that they just never do."

I nod. "My mom's like, absurdly queer positive, okay? Like, 'I'm pretty sure she's crushed that I like boys' levels of queer positive. If you ever need to hide out somewhere or just get away for a bit, she's a pretty safe adult to bug who happens to only live a few floors up."

His eyes widen. "I'm... thanks. Seriously."

I sigh. "Geez you have to stop doing that. You're welcome. Whatever. Don't make me say it again." I put on my backpack and start down the hill. "See you Monday, asshole!" I call as I go.

"See you, multiple bags worth of dicks!"

Luckily, I'm in the lead so I don't have to worry about hiding my smile.

Chapter 14

"Ugg!" I chuck a pencil at the wall. For the third time in three minutes.

Every few years, Quebec starts talking about leaving Canada. I hope they hurry up and do it soon so we can switch to just having one national language.

Mom hears my grumbling and swoops into the living room. And I do mean swoop. When she's not at work, my mom's a big fan of flowing dresses.

"French?" She guesses.

"No language should be allowed to have this many silent letters."

She bends over me to grab a chocolate covered pretzel and kisses my head on the way back up. "Agreed. Is Marn in your class? She's always been good at this stuff."

'This stuff' doesn't mean French, it means school.

"She's busy." I think I'm lying but then Mom goes,

"right, it's her cousin's birthday this weekend."

And for some reason that really bothers me. I'm supposed to have Marnie's schedule down pact. I'm supposed to feel something when she's not in town. But all I've been thinking about is French.

My mother must see something in my expression because she frowns. She sits down beside me. That means we're in talking mode. "Is everything okay with you girls?" She checks. "She hasn't been around."

I bite back my first response. That my mom hasn't been either. Now that I'm old enough to stay home alone, Mom's been picking up more shifts so our schedules basically only ever align on the occasional weekend. I'm not mad at her though. Or Marnie. It's just the French.

"We're fine. Just busier with schoolwork and stuff."

"Is that going okay?" She keeps frowning at me. "School stuff? Pia says Marnie's been making lots of friends, but it doesn't seem like—"

"I'm all good."

She opens her mouth, sighs, and closes it again. She stands up. "Maybe ask a friend then, honey. I'm awful at languages. That's where you get it from."

"Right," I say. "Smart. I'll text people."

I have the contact information for exactly one person in my French class in my phone. I go through two more mini-pencil explosions before feeling pathetic enough to text him.

> **me:** ...
>
> **me:** *did you study for the french quiz yet*

Gabe must also have no life, because the response comes back almost instantly.

> **asshole:** *Is this a trap?*
>
> **me:** *i was just gonna say u can come ovr if u wanted someone to study with*
>
> **asshole:** *You mean someone to tutor?*
>
> me: *forget it.*

My mom knocks on my bedroom door ten minutes later. I'm in the process of trying to drown my sorrows under crappy reality TV shows.

"Your friend..." She catches herself. "Gabe DeLuca's waiting for you."

I slam my laptop shut.

Mom frowns. "Do I... let him in?"

"Yes, yeah. He's good at French."

She stares for another moment before shrugging. "He's in the living room."

I triple check that I've closed all evidence of my reality show watching before walking into the living room. Gabe's sitting freakishly still on my couch.

81

"Hey," I raise a hand to wave then feel stupid for raising a hand to wave and try to stuff it into my pocket before remembering that I don't have pockets and just kind of letting it awkwardly thump against my side. Luckily, he looks even more uncomfortable.

"Your mom doesn't seem like she likes me," he hisses once I've sat down across from him.

I roll my eyes. "Yeah, well, you did get me suspended in middle school, so—"

"After you almost broke my nose!"

I shrug. "You deserved it. She gets that."

He looks towards the kitchen.

I sigh. "Mom!" I call. "You're intimidating my... boy I tricked into helping me not fail French!"

She materializes from just behind the wall. I'm half her so I should have seen that coming. "The one you made a voodoo doll of last year?"

I turn back to Gabe. "She's kidding." She's not, but it was a silly late night sleepover idea. Nothing as obsessive as she's making it sound.

Mom just winks.

"Can you go out for a bit?" I ask. "Please?"

"Oh, so now he's also—"

Gabe's entire face is red.

"Mom. Please."

She sighs. Dramatically. Because I'm half her. "Fine." She grabs her key off the counter. "I'll go do a grocery run."

"Thank you! Love ya."

She nods. "Love ya." She waves to Gabe on her way out. "Hope it was nice to see you, Gabriel."

I sigh once the door's closed. "Sorry, she's an acquired taste."

"She's always seemed nice," he shrugs.

I roll my eyes. There are plenty of ways you could describe my mother, but 'nice' never gets even close to the top of any list. It's one of my favourite things about her. I hesitate. "She just likes giving people crap. All bark no bite. The other day when I said—"

"Talk about it and I stop letting you cheat off of me in French."

My face goes hot. "You um... knew I was doing that last week?"

He rolls his eyes. "You're so unsubtle about it that I couldn't believe you didn't get caught. Just didn't say anything because I figured you'd somehow find a way to get me blamed instead."

I pick at the couch. "I'll say you didn't know, if I get caught. I mean I'll obviously try to lie my way out first but—"

"You're doing it again?"

"If I say no, will you keep forgetting to cover your work?"

He sighs. "I thought you wanted to study, Cory."

I suddenly remember that I hate him. "I officially take back every nice thing I've ever said about you."

"I don't think you've ever actually done that yet."

"You're such an asshole."

"I walked up two flights of stairs to help you study, fully told you that I let you cheat off of me, and somehow that makes me an asshole?"

"You can go. I only invited you over because my mom was acting like I was all weird and friendless or whatever."

His brow furrows. "You want to be friends?"

"Of course not," I say quickly. "I just didn't want to give her an excuse to start asking Marnie's mom too many questions and you were the closest age-appropriate person nearby. And I thought you'd be useful for once because you seemed to know how verbs worked but if that means you're going to treat me like a freaking idiot, it's not worth it. Go. Be gone."

He's quiet for a long moment before sighing. He gets up to move beside me. "Let's conjugate some irregular verbs."

I roll my eyes. "I said I didn't want help."

He shrugs. "You also said I'm supposed to be teacher adjacent one day though. Figured I should get some practice in."

I should push back more because he's definitely switched to fully offering out of pity, but I also really don't want to fail French, so I let him help.

When I've kind of gotten everything and he should go, Gabe doesn't.

"You know," he says slowly. "If you're trying to work on the friend thing—"

"We're never going to be friends," I stop him.

"We used to be."

"You're misremembering things then."

He rolls his eyes. "I was just gonna say you should join a club or something."

Obviously I've already thought of that. I hate that he doesn't think I've already thought of that. "Recruitment's already over. Maybe there'll be more stuff next semester."

"I don't know, some are still looking. I have chess club on Wednesdays and they're always—"

I burst out laughing.

"Shut up!" He whacks me with my own pillow. "I'm trying to help!"

"You're so, so lame," I manage once I catch my breath a bit more.

"Says the girl with exactly zero friends."

I wind up to hit his side and he catches my fist. Something unsettles in my stomach at that, the feeling of his fingers around my knuckles. I swallow.

"Too far?" He checks.

I groan. "Don't you dare do that and pretend you're a good person."

He releases my fingers. My stomach settles again.

"I'm guessing chess is a no go then?"

"I don't even know how to play."

"It's actually not that hard. I can—"

I can't let him stay here even longer. I can't risk a repeat of... whatever that just was. "I'm actually very okay with not knowing how to play. No offense. Or... offense, I guess."

Gabe rolls his eyes. "Well, if you keep sucking at the friendship thing then, you could always hang out with mine so you don't seem as visibly pathetic or whatever. At lunch and stuff. I've managed to trick a few people into liking me."

I squint at him, confused. Gabriel DeLuca and I are not the kind of people who help each other study just because. We're definitely not the kind of people who then offer up social invitations. There has to be some kind of angle. He's tricking me into something. He tries to stare back at me, but his eyes keep flitting to the side. He's nervous.

I realize all at once that he thinks I'm the one playing him. I sigh. "I said I wasn't going to tell anyone, Gabe," I remind him. "I meant that. You're fine."

He frowns. "What?"

"I didn't mean to... I wasn't like, ordering you to come help. With French. I'm not going to tell anyone just because you say no to something or piss me off or whatever."

"Okay?" He says slowly. "I know?"

"You don't have to try and appease me or whatever. It makes me feel pathetic and you look pathetic so... I could literally find out you're an actual supervillain or something and I still wouldn't tell anyone because it wouldn't be at all relevant to your supervillainy. I swear."

"Okay," he says again, but his knee's suddenly shaking.

I sigh. "Give me your phone."

"I don't know why you keep thinking I'm ever actually going to do that."

I roll my eyes. "Record me."

"Why?"

"Mutually assured destruction," I explain. "Just... record me, yeah?"

I wait for him to press record.

"This is my official confession that I've cheated on and plan to keep—Gabe's bi—cheating on every French quiz and test for the foreseeable future." I hit the stop button myself.

"What the hell was that?"

"Now if I out you, you have no reason not to show that to the school and screw me over too, yeah? Now you can stop worrying about it."

"Cory. I can't have a video like that on my phone."

"Oh," I realize. "Right. I umm..." I consider. "Fine," I sigh. "Record again."

I reconfess with no mention of Gabe.

"Thanks," he nods, swiping through his camera roll to presumably delete the earlier clip. "That—"

"If you show it to anyone and I haven't outed you, I will." It's a lie, obviously, but it wouldn't be a fair trade if he didn't think I meant it. Mutually assured destruction doesn't work unless it's actually mutual.

"I won't," he says. "Promise." He gets up and starts to head out. "Are you crashing my lunch group Monday? We normally sit in the science hall. Cafeteria's kind of hectic."

I feel my eyebrows shoot up. "You'd still... want me too?"

He rolls his eyes. "Wouldn't have offered if I didn't."

"I'll think about it." I've already decided, but I don't want him to get a big head about it. "But if you're messing with me and this is some kind of—"

"What could I possibly be up to?" He grins. "All you'll have to do is pretend you enjoy spending time with me for an hour and a half. Easy."

"I hate you."

He laughs. "See you Monday. I'll tell my friends to expect you."

Chapter 15

My boy crushes and girl crushes (or, crush) have always felt different. With boys (or maybe just with people who aren't Marnie) the stakes are always lower. With boys (or maybe just with people who aren't Marnie) I realize I like them, ask them out a few days later, and then even if they decline (which in my experience, they usually do) I'm over it within a week or two.

Something happened to my stomach when Gabe touched my fingers. Something that's been happening to my stomach every time I think of seeing him again.

With boys, crushes come fast and fleeting and full of confidence. Only girls (or maybe only people who are Marnie) are supposed to make me nervous. Maybe that's supposed to mean something. If I like boys and girls differently, maybe I'm not actually bi and I'm holding onto the wrong secret.

But suddenly, I am nervous. Stomach spinning nervous. Finger tapping nervous. Maybe that's just because I know how wrong this is, though. Maybe it's because I've realized that even if I don't hate Gabe anymore, maybe even if I like him, that can still be okay. Having a crush on him is not. Having a crush on him is irredeemable. Maybe he's not a homophobe or a Marnie hater or even as annoying as I remember him being, but he's still Gabriel DeLuca.

He's a boy though, so I'll be fine. Just a couple of weeks of slight awkwardness and then I'll be home free. Everything'll go back the way it was supposed to.

Marnie gets back in Monday morning which means that I'm supposed to meet Gabe in the parking garage Monday morning so that she doesn't have to see him. But when I enter the stairwell, he's pacing at the top.

I frown. "Waiting here kind of defeats not just coming to my door. You know that, right?"

He stops moving. "My mom's driving."

"Okay, cool. I figured."

"I just needed to make sure—"

"Gabe." I touch his arm. I only do it to try and stop him from moving because he's making me dizzy, but I instantly regret it. I don't know how to pull away without making it obvious that I'm desperate to pull away so we just stand there, skin touching. "Everything's fine. I'm not going to do anything stupid."

He just nods.

I sigh. "I'll be late if you let me walk now so you're stuck with me today but if this is going to be like, a thing, I can always tell her I want to start walking alone again, okay?"

Finally, he pulls away. He stuffs his hands into his pockets so I use the opportunity to do the same. "No, that's... it's fine. It'll be fine."

"It will be," I confirm. "Let me know if you change your mind though. Preferably with more than a few minutes notice next time."

Maybe, I realize, Gabe doesn't like girls at all. I can't remember him dating any in middle school. I know bisexuality's a real thing—I'm still pretty sure that might be the word I'm supposed to be using to describe myself—but I also know that Gabe didn't come out to me on purpose. Maybe "I like girls and guys" had just felt safer than "I like guys" in that moment.

And even if he does like girls, that doesn't mean that he'd ever like me. We're supposed to be the furthest thing from each other's types imaginable.

Just a couple of weeks and I'll get to be over all this.

"We'd better go," he says. And then doesn't start down the stairs.

I move past him. I turn around. "I swear it'll be fine, okay?" I promise. "There's literally no reason I'd bring anything up. It's irrelevant. Everything's still exactly the same."

"Exactly the same," he echoes.

Except my eye get caught on his lips as I watch him talk and I'm forced to remember that it isn't.

Nonymous

I've never given much thought to the kind of people Gabe would be friends with. In elementary school I think I just decided that it was boys in general and now I guess I was picturing a ton of Gabe clones or something. I was at least mostly right about the boy thing. I enter the science hall and find Gabe sitting with three guys I don't recognize and only one girl. He spots me before I have time to finish overanalyzing them.

"Cory!" He raises two fingers into the air. "Over here!" As if there's anywhere else I can possible be. I suddenly feel like the hallway's full of people staring at me but that's ridiculous because this is just Gabe and four of his (probably equally uncool and dorky) friends. I roll my shoulders back, smile, and walk towards them. I'm supposed to be the outgoing one, even when Marnie's not around.

Gabe's moved over to make space beside him, but I sit down next to the only other girl there anyway. I have nothing against boys, but I've also never really been friends with any of them outside of relatives and summer camps. I obviously know that they don't actually have cooties, but by the time I'd figured that out, I'd already classified all the guys in our elementary school as infected and crossing that line had just felt too weird. I'd only thought about boys in middle school when they were romantic interests.

(Maybe that's where all the stomach fluttering's come from. Maybe my body just doesn't know how to react to hanging out with boys platonically yet).

"Hi," I smile. "I'm Cory."

They go around and give me their names (Kenny, Damir, Sean, Amaya) and then Gabe accidentally tacks his on at the end even though everyone present already knows it, remembers that everyone knows it, and laughs awkwardly while his ears go red.

And I, unfortunately, realize that I somehow find that cute.

I dig my nails into my palm. This better not last the whole two weeks.

"How do you know Gabe?" Damir asks.

"Elementary school," I say as he responds, "she lives in my building."

Kenny smirks. He leans forward and drops his voice. "I think Gabe here might have a bit of a crush on you."

I flinch.

I wasn't born yesterday. I've been the girl people joke about their friends liking. Almost every girl has been. The difference though, is what's supposed to make it funny.

With other girls—girls with small voices and smaller bodies—the guy's supposed to get all embarrassed and tongue tied because he could probably realistically fall for a girl like that at least a little even if he knows next to nothing about her.

With girls like me, they're supposed to be embarrassed because the sheer act of liking girls like me is supposed to be embarrassing.

Normally, I'm the kind of person who calls out things like that, but it's always been one that I've never managed to put just right. Because they do it to pretty girls too, so they have plausible deniability. Even if we all know exactly what they mean.

Or maybe they really don't. Maybe Kenny said it truly believing that it was a harmless, neutral comment targeted only at messing with Gabe. Everyone moves on like it was nothing and maybe it was to them, but Gabe's blushing and not looking at me and my brain had to go form a stupid crush on him at the worst possible time because noticing that, knowing that the prospect of liking me back makes him so visibly embarrassed, makes me feel like crap.

Chapter 16

We've done Thanksgiving at the Accardi's for as long as I can remember. Not because any of us are particularly big Thanksgiving people, Pia's just a better cook and it's an excuse to get together and eat her food.

I'm pretty sure we've done Thanksgiving at the Accardi's our entire lives, but the night before, Marnie still texts me.

> **Marnie:** *You don't have to come over tomorrow, if you don't want to.*

I just stare at my phone. I want to. I need to. Maybe if I lie and say I was already asleep I can tell her it was too late to back out.

Another text comes fifteen minutes later.

> **Marnie:** *Not that I don't want you to. I want you to. Just if you're uncomfortable with it. Let me know.*

I wait another minute before responding so she hopefully won't notice that I was ignoring the initial text.

> **Me:** *we'll be there*
>
> **Me:** *ur not hogging all the food to urself*
>
> **Marnie:** *Awesome :)*
>
> **Marnie:** *I really did want you to come, for the record. Just didn't want to pressure you.*
>
> **Marnie:** *It'll be fun.*
>
> **Marnie:** *I've missed you.*

I send a smiley face and roll over with a non-digital smile on my mine to try and actually fall asleep. Maybe it really will be fun.

"Happy Thanksgiving!" Pia hugs me first. Then she's awkwardly handing me off to Marnie who waits a second too long before doing the same.

It's been just over month since school started and only three since middle school ended, but I can suddenly see the difference on her. She's half an inch taller. Her skin's going smoother. Her hair's longer and in a ponytail right now (she rarely wears it loose anymore) and her clothes have gone shorter and tighter. She's not wearing a ton of makeup but there's mascara on her eyelashes and there never used to be mascara on her eyelashes. I don't hate her for changing, I just wish that I'd been there to see all of that happening. It feels wrong realizing that we can grow without each other.

"Hey," she's smiling when she lets go of me, but it's nervous. Forced.

"Hey," my dried-out tongue echoes.

Her fingers move to mine. She leans forward. "Let's go pretend to be busy before they force us to help set up."

I smile (a bit realer this time) and let myself be dragged to her bedroom.

"So!" She hops onto her bed and pulls a pink heart pillow to her chest. That, at least, is still the same. Marnie's room's been far too pink for anyone to cope with since we were six. "How's your semester going? Catch me up."

I sit down at the foot of her bed and try to pretend it feels as normal and natural as it's supposed to. "It's fine. A lot less dramatic and exciting than I thought it would be."

"Ugg, I know. It's too much the same and too different all at the same time, you know?"

I don't know. I nod anyway. "How are your classes going?"

"Good! I really like music. I'm probably gonna go out for band next year."

"Nice."

She sighs. She bends practically in half to take my hand. "I hate this," she says. "We're not supposed to... my cousins don't even live that far away, right? It's like, less than a three-hour drive and they used to be super fun to hang out with when we were all younger but now it's like every time I see them we spend the whole time playing catch up because we don't really know each other well and it feels weird and formal and I didn't... we're not supposed to be like that."

I find a sequin on her bedspread. Flip it back and forth and back and forth.

"We're going to be best friends until we're a hundred, right? This is just some misguided experiment, but we'll go back to normal at the end of the semester and do that? We promised we would, so we have to..." she jolts. "I know I've already broken another promise but we're still—"

I smile and link my fingers through hers. "Until we're a hundred," I say. "And then for the rest of eternity if they've figured out how to plug our brains into some weird hivemind by then. Promise."

She relaxes a little. "This whole thing was so stupid. If you wanted to skip right back to—"

"We made it almost halfway through the semester," I shrug. "I'm fine with seeing it through."

It's supposed to be a lie but even as I say it, I realize that maybe it's not anymore. Maybe not fully. Sure when I see her in the hall having fun with people who aren't me I ache a little wanting to be a part of it, but I'm finally getting half decent at making friends who aren't Marnie. Pretty soon, Gabe's friends might even tolerate me on my own merit without him even being there to justify my existence.

"Oh," Marnie says. "That's... thanks. Seriously. For going along with this."

I make myself grin. "So, how's this girlfriend I've been hearing so little about?"

Marnie smiles and I realize that I hate how genuine it looks a lot less than I'd thought that I would. "Izzie's great. Really cool. She's loud and confident and funny and... she reminds me a lot of you, actually. I think you'll really like her."

That part though, definitely stings.

"Awesome," I lie.

"How are umm..." she wrings her hands together. "I notice you've been hanging out with new people too."

My fake smile falls. Of course she has. I don't know why I thought keeping him off of our floor would erase the fact that I've very publicly been hanging out with Gabe and his friends every day for the last two weeks.

"Marn, I'm..."

"You're allowed to be friends with whoever you want," she stops me, voice tight. "Seriously, I'm glad you—"

"I wouldn't even tolerate being around anyone who'd be a dick about any part of you."

She nods. "Is he... nice?"

I snort. "Absolutely not. But in a generally annoying way, not a bigoted one, I swear."

"I know," she says. "That's fine." But her fingers are still knotted together.

I sigh. "Marnie."

She chews on her lip. "I never said you couldn't be friends with him," she says. "If you were waiting for me to—"

I roll my eyes. "Marnie, I could barely stand him even before he was momentarily awful. It wasn't exactly a loss."

"Do you like him?"

I choke but luckily, she interprets it as laughter. "Absolutely not."

"I always figured you guys would get married." That, crush or not, Marnie thinking I'm straight or not, definitely doesn't feel good. "In like the little kid way where you assume everyone you know has to marry someone else you know."

I roll my eyes. Again. I hope she's somehow forgotten that it's my default cover up. "Well, you definitely don't have to worry about that happening any time soon. At least one of us is in a relationship."

She frowns. "This hasn't been me choosing a girl over you."

"I know." I do.

"I'd never... you'd come above every girl I could ever be romantically interested in, you know that, right?"

Knife. Heart.

I smile. I shift up the bed to lean against her. "Gosh you're sappy. Stop treating this like a breakup. We'll be back to normal in a couple of months, right?"

"Right," she says.

I really want to believe her. I think I actually might need to believe her. So, I pretend I don't notice how quiet her voice gets.

Chapter 17

I've been telling myself that Gabe's friends aren't actually assholes despite the occasional slightly misguided comment because that's what you do when you're a loser with no one else to talk to. But then we're talking about our long weekends and I mention spending it at Marnie's and Amaya says, "who?"

And Kenny responds with a slur.

I freeze. For some reason, my first thought is that I've misheard him. I've never heard that word out loud before. I'm not even sure where I learned it. But I must have, because it makes my whole body go hot.

I wait. I'm not sure what for. I think for someone else to say something, maybe? I've been defending Marnie our entire lives and I'll continue to do it forever, but sometimes that gets tiring. Especially if I'm also kind of gay. Especially if I'd also kind of be defending myself. I need someone to call him out so I'll know that at least someone else realizes that that wasn't okay, but the conversation's already moving on. Gabe's looking everywhere but me so I know that he's, at least, heard it too. I think that might make it worse. That he knows it's wrong (that he probably also knows that he's a big part of the reason why people like Kenny even know enough about Marnie to say stuff like that) but he's still choosing to ignore it. But isn't that also what I'm doing? Waiting for someone else to talk?

I shove my fists into my pockets. I've only punched someone once before, but if Kenny doesn't apologize immediately, I don't want it happening again. "What did—" I start.

"Dude."

At first I think Gabe's trying to stop me and my hands come flying out of my pockets again. But he's staring at Kenny.

Kenny laughs. "What did I do this time?"

"You can't just say that, stupid. It's a slur."

He rolls his eyes. "It's not like she heard it. Calm down."

"It's a slur," Gabe repeats.

His voice is nowhere near strong and he's not even looking at anyone, but Kenny's eyes still widen.

"Oh," he says. "Oh, shit. Cory, if you're—"

I'm used to it. People have always jumped to me the most likely gay person in the room, even with Marnie standing right there. "There doesn't have to be a lesbian present for that to not be okay, asshole."

Someone (Damir, I think) goes "ooh."

Kenny puts his arms up in surrender. "Calm down, it's no big—"

I get up. "I'm leaving."

"Cory." Someone (Amaya, I think) tries to stop me.

"If that kind of thing's no big deal here, I'm leaving."

No one follows me.

Friday's not until tomorrow so we have no questions to answer, but instead of letting me walk up to my apartment on my own, Gabe says, "see you later, school stuff," and follows me out of his mom's car.

"Cory."

I keep walking.

"Cory!"

I'm not even mad at him specifically but I keep walking anyway. If he catches up, he'll want me to reassure him that we're fine so he can feel better about himself. I'm sick of always having to be the one to clear other people's consciousness.

"Cory!"

I take a chance. The universe finally works in my favor and the elevator opens. I slam my finger against the close door button, but he sticks out a foot just in time, the sensor catches it, and they open again.

I frown. "You really have to stop sticking your leg in doorways."

He sighs. "Cory."

And I wait for it. The "are you mad?" followed inevitably by the "I'm really sad that you're mad" and the "please stop being mad now, okay? Tell me how great I am."

He says exactly what I thought he would too. The same words, just rearranged. "You're mad."

It's barely a difference but it still is one, so I falter. I swallow down the denial I'd been planning on giving because something about hearing it spoken makes me realize, "yeah, I am."

He winces. "I'm sorry that happened. I don't like, actively seek out slightly homophobic friends, for the record."

"No, that must just be a side effect of letting people be homophobic around you."

"I didn't... I told him it wasn't okay."

"Do you want a freaking award? It doesn't matter what you said, you still stayed. That was you telling him you were okay with it."

He fixes his hair. "I'm not... obviously I'm not planning on—"

The elevator opens. I step off. "I have to go."

"Cory." He grabs at me. "Obviously I'm not planning on hanging out with him anymore. I just couldn't—"

"I've got to go."

"Come on, you have to get why—"

"Let go of me!" I scream. He does. "You're such an asshole, you know that? You're such an asshole and you can't keep just apologizing for things after the fact and expect that to make everyone forget how awful of a person you are! That's not how it works."

"I'm—"

He's not even holding onto me, but for some reason I repeat, "let me go!"

He steps back into the elevator. He's not the person I'm actually mad at (maybe it's Kenny. Maybe it's Marnie. Maybe it's just me) but he steps back into the elevator and I let him.

Nonymous

    I know that it's not his fault. But he was practically offering himself up as something I could yell at and I've spent all semester keeping myself from doing that. It felt good to be loud again.

Chapter 18

"Today," Mr. McCoy announces. "We're working one on one with our scene partners. I want everyone sitting facing each other, knees touching."

I find Gabe. Who rode all the way to school in silence while I talked to his mom. I should probably apologize for yelling at him, but that feels too close to pulling my anger back in again.

He watches his own fingers tap against the floor.

"I want you all to practice your lines back and forth. For the whole period."

"Hi," I say first.

"Hi," he mumbles.

Other groups get really into it. They're on their feet screaming at each other. They laugh and cry and work through every emotion named and otherwise. We stay on the floor.

"Hi."
"Hi."
"Hi."
"Hi."
"Hi."
"Hi."
"Hi."
"Hi."

It's over an hour of hellos. I'm uncomfortable with how close they all start to sound to goodbyes.

Chapter 19

I love Marnie. I do. I've loved her my entire life, so obviously I don't want her to ever have to be upset.

I think I just also hate having to be the one who's always fine?

I was the one who got typecast as loud when we were kids because I was bigger and more outgoing and impulsive, but Marnie has always been the one who's emotions got to be big.

It was the kind of thing I just grew up hearing.

"Yes, I know you want to stay and play, but Marnie's having some big emotions right now so we have to go home."

"Can't you just do what Marnie wants? You know she'll get all upset if you don't."

I've lived my entire life by Marnie's emotions and it's not like I resent her for it. I would never have wanted to trap her in situations that would've made her upset just because that was what I would have preferred to do. But I just wish it was something she'd noticed more? Or that anyone had noticed more?

The moms always expected it. It's never "look at how nice Cory's being," or "look how careful she's being". I can't remember being praised for it even once even though it was so clearly what they were expecting me to do. And Marnie didn't know and Marnie was never doing it on purpose and maybe I'm an asshole for remembering Marnie in distress and only thinking about how difficult that was for me, but it sucked, sometimes. Which wasn't her fault, but it also wasn't mine.

I'd protect Marnie from anything. I still will. I just wish that that didn't mean having to pretend that I don't need protecting sometimes too. Because Marnie's emotions were always bigger, but that didn't mean that mine weren't also there. I just learned how to make them smaller around her so she'd have enough space for her own.

Nonymous

Since we're still avoiding my floor (even though Marnie's texted twice now to say that it's really, really okay if we don't) I'm supposed to meet Gabe at the front of the school to work through our weekly questions every Friday. When I get there, his mom's already pulled in.

I slow down as I approach. "I'm so sorry, totally forgot," I lean down to say through the window. "I have to pick up some stuff for a project for another class from the plaza. I don't need a ride today." I turn to Gabe. "Wanna walk with and we'll get our work done on the way? Or I can come to yours after?"

He watches me carefully. "Might as well walk." He pats a hand against the top of the car. "Sorry, Mom. thanks for coming."

She smiles. "No problem! Enjoy the sun. You guys have fun."

And then we're alone.

"Are you okay with us working at your place now?" I ask, already walking towards the plaza. "We still shouldn't do mine. Or did you somehow forget we have a couple of probably slightly too personal for school questions to answer?" I know the real answer probably isn't either of those options, but my current plan is to move forward like nothing happened.

"There's only one this week, I already checked. We can do it Monday before class if you need more space. Or even—"

I sigh. "Gabe. We're fine. We were fine. I'm... I'm pissed at her I think, okay? That wasn't about you. Obviously that was an uncomfy, stressful situation for you too and you like, barely fucked up. You almost did everything perfectly, actually. I'm..." I grit my teeth. Squeeze my fists. "I'm sorry."

"What did she do?" He asks. "If you want to—"

"Nothing. Or... cut me off, I guess, but she's super apologetic but always 'please don't be mad' at me apologetic so somehow I always end up being the one comforting her?"

Gabe nods. "Maybe tell her you're mad?"

I sigh. "I can't just... it's not even her fault. If I'd told her from the beginning she wouldn't have even... it's fine. I don't want to talk about it."

"I'd want to know," he says. "Whenever you're pissed at me. Or... hate me more than usual, I guess. I know you're always at least kind of pissed."

I roll my eyes. "Shut up. You know I'm not actually... we're friends now. Kind of."

He beams, leaning to the side to hit my shoulder with his. "I know. Just wanted to hear you say it first."

"Asshole." Except, I can't even pretend I believe it anymore because even through at least four layers of clothing, my shoulder's still warm from when his brushed against it. I kick at a chunk of cement to give myself something else to look at.

It's been more than two weeks. I don't know what that means.

Nonymous

Chapter 20

I spend the next week spending way too much time alone with Gabriel DeLuca for it to possibly be healthy. We ride to school together and ride home together whenever he doesn't have clubs. We were already eating lunch together but since we're both protest-ditching his friends, it feels a lot more improper suddenly. I'm not alone with him. Not really. We eat in the cafeteria surrounded by other people and most of the time at least one of us is spending more time on course work than talking to the other person, but it still feels too close to isolated.

Every day, I make sure I have at least three pencils and a sharpener in my bag. He offered me one on Monday and I was too terrified that our hands would brush as he handed it over to accept it so now, I always make sure I have at least three pencils ready to go.

I'm not supposed to get shy around crushes (unless they're Marnie, but she's the exception to every single rule) and I don't technically get shy around him either. But I do get nervous. If he were any other guy and we were in middle school I would have already asked him out and he would have let me down gently which would make me beyond pissed because Gabe and I have never once been gentle with each other but then he'd be making me feel pissed instead of mushy and everything would go back to being alright.

I don't want to be pissed at him though. I like riding to school together and walking to class together and being assholes together and even just being silent together. Maybe that was what had always made Marnie feel so different. Maybe it had nothing to do with her being a girl crush. Having crushes on people is infinitely more difficult when you actually like them first.

We don't have any drama homework on Friday because Mr. McCoy proclaims that Halloween is "theatre kid Christmas" and that he wants to give all of us time to celebrate. But when I walk out front and Gabe waves me over, there isn't a car in sight.

"She must be late," he says before I can even ask what's going on. "Probably forgot we weren't walking home today. I'm supposed to pick up last minute Halloween candy so you can walk, wait here yourself, or—"

I hit his arm. "You're so annoying."

"Well if you'd reminded me that we needed a ride home I could've texted her earlier and—"

"Give me your phone."

He sighs. "Stop doing that."

"Why? Because you knew we didn't have any work to do and told your mom not to come get us anyway because you're obsessed with hanging out with me?"

He rolls his eyes but his ears go red, so I know that I'm right. "I didn't say you had to come with," he mumbles. "You can always go home by yourself."

"I don't have anything better to do. I'm always down for candy, just ask me like a normal person next time though."

He sighs. "You wouldn't have said yes if I'd asked you like a normal person, Cory."

"Not—"

"I've literally never gotten you to hangout with me without giving you an excuse to use first. It's insufferable."

"I don't do that."

"You absolutely do."

"Ask then," I shrug. "See what I say."

He sighs. "Will you, Cory Murphy, come buy overpriced chocolate with me so I don't have to lug it all back on my own?"

I roll my eyes. "Okay, in what world was that not also coming up with an excuse? We're both dysfunctional. It's why we—"

I try to move past him but he grabs my arm. "Come get Halloween candy because for some reason I really like hanging out with you then."

I freeze. I blink. I swallow.

My laugh is light and breathy and far girlier than I've ever remembered it sounding. "Fine, whatever. You didn't have to beg."

There's nothing but candy corn left at the grocery store because most people don't wait until the day before Halloween to do their candy shopping, so we walk all the way to the one near the elementary school, but there's none there either.

Gabe sighs. "Okay, full disclosure, I was supposed to pick this up weeks ago."

"Yeah, I kind of figured."

"It's not my fault! We normally have stuff to do on Fridays and I got distracted last time."

I think I like that, being a distraction. I think I really, really like that.

I need to remind myself that I don't though, so I continue on to the corner store.

Mr. T's helping someone else when we enter so I don't have to worry about him asking where Marnie is, but I still instantly lose the ability to hear anything Gabe's saying the moment the door closes behind us.

I didn't grow up here. I grew up in hallways and classrooms and bedrooms. Parks and camps and hotels. It would be stupid to say that we grew up in a corner store, but we learned to be independent here. We learned to be independent together here.

Marnie would keep track of how much we were spending and I would talk her into trying whatever new candy I'd decided that we absolutely had to try that day. I'd talk to Mr. T and she'd count out our change. I can't remember the last time I was here without Marnie.

Corner store candy's more expensive than bulk grocery store candy, but Gabe manages to find a couple of hundred packs of lollipops while I numbly follow him around. We make it to the counter and I'm looking down because something about being here's already way too overwhelming but then Mr. T says "Cory!" because he always does, and I have to talk because I was always the one who talked to adults.

I smile. "How are you?"

"Good! Where's your friend?"

"Busy," I feel my forehead go wrinkly and smooth it out. "We're in high school now."

"Good for you guys."

He rings up Gabe's stuff. We almost make it out the door.

"Oh, Cory!" He reaches beneath the counter. "Almost forgot. We changed inventory a bit. Put some aside for you girls."

He slides a small bag with ten HunGums in it across the counter. I just stare.

"You're not... stocking them anymore?"

He laughs. "I don't think anyone else has bought them for years. The price just went up, so..."

I swallow. "Right," I fish around in my pocket. "Right, how much..."

He waves off the question. "On me. Have a good Halloween."

I know that it's not our fault. I know that we weren't singlehandedly keeping HunGums profitable and that he likely would have stopped stocking them whether or not we were still buying them weekly. But for a moment, it feels like it is. For a moment, I want to find Marnie and scream at her for ruining this for me.

Instead, I say 'thank you', slip the box into my pocket, and speedwalk out of the store.

Chapter 21

"I wasn't actually going to force you to carry things, you know," Gabe catches up with me.

I hadn't meant to leave without him. I'd just momentarily forgotten that he existed.

"I mean, I was," he admits. "But if I'd known it would have made you run away, I would've just asked for a bag from the get go. I'm not actually as weak as I look."

"Ha," I manage.

"What was that all about anyway? I didn't realize you were corner store royalty. Should have used you for a discount or something. What's—"

"I don't want to talk to you right now!"

We both stop moving.

"I'm..." I start, but I don't know how to say it. That I'm so fragile that something as small as a candy I don't even like the taste of going out of stock is making my whole world physically blurry. That I'm so obsessed with her that the world's off kilter now but I'm still too stubborn to tell her that I need her to help me set it right again. "I actually don't feel like doing anything, right now," I decide. "I'll... see you Monday."

I make my legs work long enough to stumble my way to a bench. I'm still aware enough to know that Gabe's sat down beside me, but not present enough to get mad about it. I stare at the sky and wait for my brain to shake itself back into order.

"Cory." Eventually, there's something hovering in front of my face. "Lollipop."

I shake my head. "Don't want it."

"You have to take it. Because I want one and I'll look like an ass if anyone sees me eating one alone."

"You can just go. I'm fine."

He holds it so close that the plastic wrapper scratches against my nose. "Lollipop."

I sigh and accept it. I leave it still against my tongue until there's no candy left on the stick.

"Cherry's my favourite," I say even though I can barely taste it anymore.

"Want another?"

"No. It's just... it is."

He nods. "I know. Grew up with you, remember? You tend to keep track of the people who'll trade you for candy that tastes like medicine."

"I couldn't stand you when we were kids," I admit. "I can't even specifically remember why."

Gabe shrugs. "That's fine. I can barely stand you now so it's not like I can judge."

I hit his shoulder.

"You good now?" He checks.

"I never said you had to stay."

He sighs. "Jesus, Cory. I'm just trying to ask if you want to talk about it."

"I'm not the kind of person who needs to do that. I'm fine. I'm over it."

"Okay, whatever. Guess I'll—" He stands up to go and lollipops go flying out all over the sidewalk. "Crap." He drops to his knees to try and scramble to pick them up even as more keep spilling from the bag.

"You tore a hole through the bag and didn't think that would cause any problems?"

"You could help, you know," he mutters.

I laugh, following him down to the ground. I'm supposed to keep laughing as we sweep them all back towards the bag but at some point it gets caught my throat and comes out the wrong way and suddenly I'm crying. Either Gabe doesn't notice, or he's doing a really good job at pretending that he hasn't noticed. He manages to genuinely convince me that he hasn't until he finally gets all the lollipops back under the control and leans back against the bench to offer me another one. I'm already feeling slightly pathetic, so I accept it.

I stick it in my mouth. I take it out. "The stuff he gave me? The candies? They're this disgusting things Marnie and I used to buy with our allowances every Sunday. We had this whole promise making ritual centered around them. And now I only have ten."

"You could probably order them online," he points out.

"That's not... it wouldn't be the same though. The point was how easy they were for us to access them, you know? That wouldn't... yeah, maybe. I might look into it."

I watch the sky for a bit.

I miss her," I admit. "Which is stupid because she's literally just down the hall from me at pretty much any given moment and all I'd have to do to get her back in my life again is tell her that I need her there, but I can't."

"I could," Gabe offers.

It's so absurd that I'm pretty sure I pull something in my neck when I turn to stare at him.

"Okay," he concedes. "Yeah, maybe not. But... I can text her from your phone? Pretend to be you, if you want."

I sigh. "That's not even... I'm not even nervous about it? I don't think. I just know if I tell her that we'll go back to normal and I'll have to spend forever wondering if she actually wants to be around me or if she's pretending for my sake?"

He rolls his eyes. "She definitely wouldn't be pretending. You guys have always been way too codependent."

I suck on the lollipop for a few more seconds. "You've known me for practically ever, right? Was there ever anything... have I changed? Is there something about me that makes me unlikable? Or even if it's not a change, I need to know what... is there?"

Gabe raises an eyebrow. "You're asking me to tell you all of my least favourite things about you?"

"Shut up," I mumble on impulse, hitting his knee with mine. Then, I consider. "Actually... yes, actually. Do that."

He throws back his head and groans. "Jesus, Cory. You're the worst."

"Right," I prompt. "But in what specific—"

"None of them," he looks right at me. "Okay? I can't think of a single thing to complain about which is actually really embarrassing, so thanks for that. You're actually..." he runs a hand through his hair. "Geez, you're a lot more tolerable than I thought you would be when we were kids, okay? If Marnie doesn't think you're cool, that's on her."

I feel my face go hot. There is absolutely no way to respond to something like that. "I'd like it if you stopped lying to me about texting your mom," I decide on.

He laughs. "Noted. What else?"

"Nothing," I shrug.

"That's it?"

"That's it."

He sticks his lollipop back into his mouth. It's hard not to look at someone's lips when you're eating candy. That must be why his eyes are also on mine.

"Well," he pushes himself to his feet. "You want the broken bag or the sealed one? Turns out I probably can't get these home on my own after all."

"Broken," I volunteer. "Clearly you can't be trusted with it."

We take the elevator up together. I offer to get off at his floor to help him get the candy to his apartment, but once I balance the bag on top of his, he swears he's got it.

"Thanks for the help," he says before going. "Again."

I shrug. "Thanks for the lollipops."

He stays there for a moment, one leg on solid ground, one in the elevator. I know there's a sensor to keep the doors from crushing him, but my eyes fly to the hold door button, just in case.

"Cory?" He says.

"Yeah?"

He's not smiling but then all of the sudden, he is. Big and stretched and fake. "Have a good Halloween."

I don't know what he was really going to say. I don't know what I was planning to respond to the thing that he was really going to say. But for hours, long after I've left the elevator, I feel my organs rising.

Chapter 22

Everything's awful, I've officially liked Gabe for almost a month now, and I still haven't figured out what to do about that.

He doesn't like me back. I know that. He's nice (sometimes, he's mostly still an ass but that's one of my favourite thing about him), but he's niceish to most people. He's also funny and smart and pretty and boys who are funny and smart and pretty don't fall for girls like me.

That's why I don't find out from the gossip mill or even from Marnie herself, but from him.

asshole: *Heads up, pretty sure Marnie just got dumped*

Because even though I've been careful not to say anything overtly romantic, it'd be difficult for me to talk about Marnie with anyone without them catching on to the fact that I'm in love with her. Because he doesn't like me back so now that she's available, he's being a good wingman. Because we're just friends.

I'm sick of always being people's "just friends".

There's no time to overanalyze the text though. Marnie might not be the person I actively have the biggest crush on, but she's still Marnie. She'll still always matter more than everything. I don't know if she wants me close or far away but I still have to try. I open my door to go knock on hers and jump back when I find her already facing me, hand frozen in the air.

"Hey," she says. It's only one word, but her voice cracks in the middle. "I'm sorry, I know I can't keep—"

I pull her into a hug. It feels good to finally be hugging her again. I should feel guiltier for reveling in that than I do. "Come in."

I leave her on the couch to go boil some hot water to make two cups of soup. When I returned, she's already unfolded a blanket and buried herself beneath it. Marnie likes to be warm inside and out when she's upset. I hand her the cup.

"Thanks," she says.

I nod.

Marnie sniffs, rubbing at her tear-streaked face. "I have to stop doing this," she says. "I can't keep showing up and—"

"Marn." I touch her knee. "If you need me, I'm here, okay? I want to be."

"You too," she says. "You still know that, right? If you ever need anything—"

"I know," I lie. "I just haven't. I've been great." I pull my legs up onto the couch. "Are we 'Izzie sucks and we're going to take up witchcraft just to figure out how to curse her' right now or more 'Izzie's still great and we're sad and need to cry about it'?"

"You heard already," she realizes.

I wince. "I didn't mean to... I'm sure it's no big deal. Gabe heard from someone and texted me. But she's a band kid and you're practically a band kid and he's close with a few band kids, so I'm sure everyone's not randomly invested in some ninth grade drama."

She starts nodding then keeps swaying. Her nails tap against her mug. "Do you like me?"

"Don't be stupid, I'm obsessed with you. We're best friends."

"But if we hadn't been," she alters. "If you hadn't known me forever and didn't feel obligated to, would you still like me?"

I frown. "Yeah, of course."

"Why?"

I think. I think of a million inappropriate answers.

She sighs. "I'm sorry, that wasn't fair to—"

"I think you're one of the nicest people I know," I stop her. "Not even in the annoying way. I would have called you out on it if it was in the annoying way. You're just genuinely nice and you care about people so, so much. And you're crazy smart. Like scary smart, sometimes. And—"

"I think I've been trying to be you," she blurts out. "Since I was like eight."

"Well that's just stupid, you're infinitely cooler."

She shakes her head. "No, I wanted... I wanted to be you. So badly. And I thought... I mean I knew that I wasn't doing a great job at it because everyone wouldn't shut up about how different we were, but I kept trying anyway and I thought that was why... I had a really good summer."

I bite down on my cheek. "That's great, Marn."

"I thought it was because you weren't there for me to copy or hide behind or something and I was funnier and more self-assertive and I even felt prettier but maybe that was all... Izzie flipped out at me? Because I think I've been doing that to her too? Trying to turn into her? But I don't know... I don't think I know how to get close to anyone without wanting to be them and I don't know if I've ever actually been myself since we were eight and I don't know how... I'm not even that upset that she's done with me, more just frustrated that now I don't know who to be anymore? And I don't know how... I don't know who. I don't know how. And I want to, but I don't know how to know either. You know?"

Technically speaking, I don't. Marnie somethings gets more difficult to keep track of when she's upset so technically, I don't know exactly what she's saying but somehow, I do. I've known her long enough that sometimes it feels like we're reading each other's minds.

"We're fourteen, Marnie," I remind her. "We have time to figure out—"

"I want to have it figured out now!" She slams her fists against the cushion. Soup spills over the edge of her cup. "Sorry," she quickly puts it down, moving the blanket to the side and attempting to pat it dry. "Sorry, I–"

I catch her fists. "You're fine," I promise. "I spill things here at least weekly. It adds to the aesthetic."

She musters up a watery smile. "I love you so much," she says. "That's why I couldn't... I love you so much that I knew that if I let myself be around you again, I'd put all my energy back into being you again. I'm so, so, sorry. I didn't mean to—"

"You're fine," I repeat. "We're all good."

She sits up a little taller. "I have a countdown, you know," she says. "On my phone? To when semester two starts and we get to go back to normal?"

I force a smile. Maybe I was a bad person for hoping that her getting dumped would send her running back to me, but if being a bad person means I'd get Marnie back, I'd be okay with that. But she's right back on track. "Oh, cool," I say. "I might set one up too."

"I miss you so much."

I squeeze my fists together. Now is not the time. "Then we'd better hurry up and finish off the semester, right? If you need anything in the meantime though, you can—"

"I won't." She stands up.

I frown. That can't be it. She can't be done with us again already. "Marn, you have like half a cup of soup left. You don't have to—"

"I think I should?" She says. "I'll work on the being me thing for real this time, okay? No hyper fixating on anyone and accidently turning into them instead. Perfect opportunity."

"Right." I get up to open the door for her. Marnie still has her own key, somewhere. She used to come and go without me even knowing she'd been by sometimes. But now, we feel a lot more formal. "See you then, I guess."

And then, again, she's gone.

And then, again, I let her go.

Chapter 23

"Okay, question two: what are your plans for semi-formal at the end of the month?"

It's just weird enough of a question that I fully believe Mr. McCoy wrote it. "Probably stay home and sulk? I don't really see the point in paying to go unless you have a date or tons of friends or something."

It's not as self-deprecating as I'm sure Mr. McCoy will interpret it. We're three months into the semester and I sometimes hang out around Gabe's newer chess-club adjacent friends, but I've always been the kind of person who just needs one person to hangout with constantly instead of half a dozen people to try and keep track of.

"What if you didn't?"

I sit up. Now that isn't colder out, I've given in and we're meeting in my apartment again. I've taken to lying down on the couch while we talk. That way, he can't sit on the same one as me. That way, I have an excuse to never look too directly at his eyes.

I've had an unshakable crush on Gabriel Deluca for two and a half months and soon, it's bound to destroy me.

"What?" I ask.

Gabe rolls his eyes. "That wasn't a real drama question, stupid. My friends are all going and most of them are bringing people. Wanna be my date?"

For a moment, I feel like a different kind of girl. The kind who understands clothes and makeup and whose laughter sparkles instead of booms. For a second, my insides turn to glitter. But then I remember that I'm not. That this isn't real. You don't seriously ask people out with 'wanna be my date?'

I've managed to pry the names of exactly three crushes out of Gabe these last few months, and they've all been guys. If he really is bi, he's probably the same kind I am. Skewing almost all the way in one direction.

I'd go anyway, because he's my friend and friends help friends stay in the closet. If it wasn't for her. I wish I was still lying down so I wouldn't have to watch him watch me plan out my answer.

"I think... I can't do that to Marnie."

"Oh," he nods. "Right."

"If... she says she's fine with us being friends and maybe she is but if we're tricking everyone into thinking that we're going out I think I'd need her to know the truth? Not that you need to tell her, obviously. Totally up to you. I swear I'd be extremely honoured to be your beard if it didn't mean lying to her."

Gabe just frowns.

"Relax, you're not actually that socially relevant. If you show up without a date I'm sure the world won't explode."

He rolls his eyes. "I was just trying to get ahead of the mob of girls who are probably just waiting to ask me."

I snort. "Sure."

"You can still come, you know," he says. "Like, openly platonically? Or on your own? Could be fun."

"I'm very okay with not spending the night surrounded by a bunch of sweaty teenagers I don't even know. You'll just have to stop by after and fill me in on anything dramatic so I can still feel relevant."

Gabe smiles. "Deal."

Chapter 24

I'm going to go to the stupid school dance.

It's not that I want to. I've managed to spend most of December fully avoiding everyone getting all excited about our first high school dance. But then a few days before the night in question I walk into the stairwell and find Marnie sniffling, and I somehow instantly know that no matter where this conversation goes, it's going to lead me to a school dance.

"Hey," I sit down beside her.

She blows out snot when she laughs. I find a tissue in my bag and hand it to her. "I swear I wasn't planting myself somewhere for you to find me," she says. "This time."

"I know." I wrap my arm around her and pull slightly until her head lands where it belongs on my shoulder. "Turns out I'm just really good at finding you."

She grabs my hand and lets her eyes fall shut. I know that she's not ignoring me, though. Marnie does that sometimes when she's collecting her thoughts. "I'm such a mess," she whispers. "This whole year, I've been..."

"Kind of, yeah." She snorts again, but I'm not quite sure I'm kidding.

"It's... there's that stupid dance, right? And I barely even like dances but high school dances felt so important a few months ago. We... I'd literally already bought a dress. We went dress shopping in September because we thought we were saving money or something and obviously my mom knows we broke up but she keeps insisting I go anyway and I can't... that'd be pathetic, right? Going on my own in a dress she helped me pick out?"

I swallow. "If you really miss her, maybe you can—"

"I don't!" Marnie says. "That's the thing, I seriously don't. Because maybe she was right and I never actually wanted to be with her and just wanted..." she sighs. "I don't know. Again. Mess."

I stand up. I hold out a hand. "Come to semi-formal with me."

"I... what?"

"Come to semiformal with me," I repeat. "It's almost the end of the semester anyway, right? Plus, this way we both get to look way cooler and popular than either of us actually are."

She frowns. "Cory, you don't have to... aren't you going with Gabe?"

I laugh. "There isn't a single universe where I'm romantically involved with Gabriel DeLuca, okay? He's... fun, but he's still Gabe." She still hasn't taken my hand, so I grab it myself and pull her up. "And we're us. Come to semiformal with me. Please."

She giggles. "I... yes. Yeah."

I beam. "Yeah?"

"That actually sounds really, really fun."

Chapter 25

The moms are ecstatic. Mine hadn't said anything to me directly about Marnie's sudden disappearance from our apartment, but I'm sure they've had dozens of late night phone calls about it. They go all out. They take the day off of work and we both take the last period the day off and are driven from mall beauty bars to salons for pedicures back to my place so my mom can do our hair.

 I kind of hate it. I haven't gotten to casually hangout with Marnie for months now and I'd been looking forward to messing up each other's hair and makeup until we were both giggling heaps. If I'm going to use the day to get us back to being us, that's a lot harder to do with other people around constantly. But I'll have the dance. And every day after. So I let us be pampered because Marnie seems to like it and today is all about making her feel better. I'm not the one who went through a recent breakup.

 She's stunning. She's always stunning, of course, but in her mall-counter makeup with her hair piled in braids on top of her head and her loose pink dress that flows as she moves, you can tell that she knows she's stunning and she's suddenly so much more overwhelming. My dress was not newly bought. It's navy and form fitting yet modest and absolutely the kind of thing that could double as professional wear if the need ever arises. Mom and Pia both individually offered to bring me dress shopping, but Mom and Pia are both thin and will never quite get what that means to me. Marnie could have walked into any dress shop and chosen whatever kind of dress she wanted. She could have been a princess or sexy or fun or modest or anywhere in between. I did the whole formal dress shopping thing last year for grad. Sometimes you don't want to spend an entire weekend going from shop to shop watching salesgirls pull out dress after dress that for some reason always look a few decades away from modern as they debate over which one will cover the most of your body. I don't think I'd even actually want to go for princess or sexy, but it's also not fun being reminded that my greatest fashion aspirations are supposed to be concealment.

It works anyway. This way, we're blue and pink, just like we were when we were kids. Marnie gets to be girly and I get to be everything that doesn't quite fit that. We're us.

They make us take a billion pictures before we go then follow us all the way down the elevator. The hall they've rented is literally just down the street from us and we've told them that we won't need rides about a million times already, but I'm still relieved and surprised when the moms actually stick to their word and stop following us in the parking lot. Marnie's holding up her skirt with one hand to keep it from getting destroyed by the snow, so I grab her other.

"Ready?" I check.

"Ready."

And we go.

Marnie's made the mistake of wearing heels. She keeps saying that that's kind of an unavoidable part of wearing long dresses, but it was still definitely a mistake.

"Marn!" I throw out my arm to catch her waist when she slips on a patch of ice. Again. We have to walk on the road to keep from destroying our shoes but unfortunately that also means that there's a lot of black ice to watch out for.

We both giggle as she regains her balance. "Almost there," she says.

That just makes me laugh more. It should only be a five minute walk, but we've somehow only shuffled a quarter of the way there in ten. "We can text the moms," I remind her again. "Guarantee they're probably waiting for us to."

She shakes her head. "I've got this."

I roll my eyes. "Who the heck plans on wearing heels for an entire night before making sure they actually know how to walk in them?"

"I wasn't planning on the dance floor being covered in ice!" She gasps as she loses her footing again and I pull her against my side. Marnie smiles. "Thanks for always catching me," she says. "Even when I kind of suck."

I shrug. "Figured I owe you after years of being the clumsy one."

Marnie frowns. "I wasn't just talking about—"

"I know," I stop her. "You're welcome."

The next time she slips, she almost takes me down with her. "You might end up having to carry me the rest of the way there," she admits. "I'd give it a fifty-fifty shot I fall and twist my ankle before we get there."

I roll my eyes. "If you hurt yourself, I'll stand by incredibly supportively while the paramedics carry you."

We show up late, shivering, but in one piece. That means it's worth it. I would've worn heels too if I'd known that it would buy us more time even if it would've landed us on our asses in the snow.

"I've got coats," I grab them and start to head towards the coat check but then Marnie's suddenly squeezing my wrist, staring out at the dance floor.

I smile. "We've got coats," I correct.

We're late so we find seats at a table of twelfth graders who ignore us the whole time instead of with anyone from our own grade, but that ends up being perfect. Neither Marnie nor I are exactly brimming with friends. We find a deck of cards and play a few rounds of speed, but her eyes keep wandering to the dance floor and I can't tell if she's nervous or excited.

"Want to dance?" It's an actual question, not an invitation. I hope that she knows that.

Marnie chews at her lip. "We shouldn't... people'll think things, Cor."

I roll my eyes. "Girl's dance with their friends all the time. And it's not even a slow song."

She shakes her head. "I'm out though. You don't get to do that while you're out. People will—"

I sigh and stand up. "Come on. Let's dance."

She frowns. "You sure? People might..."

I roll my eyes. "Marn, I'm a girl with a boy's name who literally only hangs out with a lesbian and a platonic guy friend. If people don't already think I'm gay, dancing with you's not going to change that."

She nods. "Alright then."

We dance. It's more jumping than dancing. Just moving with the wave of other teenagers. We keep our hands clasped between us, but our actual bodies are still pretty far apart and I need to keep it that way. I really can't afford to have two unattainable crushes right now. That'd have to be playing into some kind of awful bisexual stereotypes and I refuse to be so bad at being a queer person that I start failing the community before even fully figuring out if I'm part of it. We last three songs. Even though every time anyone gets close enough to brush against Marnie her grip on my fingers goes tight and she practically jumps out of her skin. Because every time I lean forward to ask "wanna stop?" she lies and says "no."

I cut it off at song number four. "Come on," I start tugging her off the dance floor.

She shakes her head. "We're having fun. We can—"

"You're definitely not having fun."

Marnie sighs, but she doesn't deny it. "We have to stay until dinner at least," she says. "It was crazy overpriced. We're not missing that."

"Then we'll find somewhere to wait."

I lead her out into the hall where we don't have to worry about people randomly bumping into us. I leave her there for a moment and go back for her coat, just in case she decides that she needs to be warm right now.

Marnie sighs when she sees me return with it. "It's not your job to take care of me, you know."

I roll my eyes. "Pretty sure that's exactly my job."

"You're barely older."

"You know that's not what I meant."

She pulls her knees into her chest and drapes the jacket over them. "Do we hold each other back, Cor? Or... not each other. Do I..."

"Don't be stupid."

"I'm not, though! Our whole lives I've—"

"I would've flunked out of like half of my classes without you, Marnie. I probably would have literally been held back."

"You could've just gotten a tutor or something."

"A tutor who could bribe me to do fractions with candy and board games and do all our favourite movie character voices whenever we had to read anything? Absolutely not."

"A normal tutor would've been able to dance with you."

"I'm pretty sure that would've at best been a breach of some kind of tutor code. At worst it would've been wildly inappropriate."

She sighs. "I'm serious, Cory. I know I'm not... I might not be good at being a teenager, but that doesn't mean I'm still a little kid. You don't have to keep protecting me from everything."

I shrug. "That's my job."

"No, it's not."

I pick at the nail polish on my fingers. White, to compliment the dress. It doesn't suit me. Maybe I'll be able to get all of it off before we have to go back in. "I've been mad at you," I make myself admit. "Really mad, I think."

She frowns. "You said you weren't—"

"I was lying. I went home that first day and destroyed my bedroom then cried while I put everything back together again then destroyed it again, just to have something to do."

Her brow pinches. "I don't... you don't do stuff like that. I'm the one who—"

"I do though, Marnie. Just not around other people. That's me lying too."

"I'm so sorry," Her eyes start to water.

I wince. "It's okay," I squeeze her shoulder. "You didn't do anything wrong. You—"

"Stop doing that!" She exclaims. "Stop trying to take care of me all the time! This isn't..." She furiously scrubs at her face. "I don't know why I'm like this. I'm not trying to be like this. It's not fair that you have to deal with me crying literally right after saying that you're mature enough not to do that around other people."

I sigh. "You're not immature, Marnie. You're—"

"Stop it!"

I nod.

She pulls a hair tie off her wrist and starts twisting it around her fingers. "I don't want to hold you back," she says. "I've always been so scared of holding you back."

"You're not—"

"I do, though. We had that grad trip last year, right? To Ottawa? And you didn't go because I didn't think I'd be able to handle being away from home for that long."

I roll my eyes. "I didn't go because I wanted to spend the week with you."

"Right, but you would've rather spent the week with me in Ottawa."

I hesitate. "That's not... it was one trip that probably would've been pretty boring anyway. It's not—"

"It wasn't though. It was field trips and dances and friendships and maybe even boyfriends and I can't keep... I'm not good at being a teenager, Cory. It's all too big and confusing and I don't think I'm ever going to be that good at it, but you could be. I'm sick of making you miss milestones because of me and this was supposed to finally be your chance to get to do all of that but here I am still messing that up and—"

I flinch. "Wait, this all... you got rid of me," I say slowly. "Because you thought that'd make me what? Have a better time in high school?"

She shrugs, eyes still trapped on her hair elastic. "It was my turn to start making sacrifices for you."

I kick her foot with mine. "Holy crap, Marnie! That's... I take back every single time I've ever called you smart, yeah? That was stupid. That was so, so stupid."

She frowns. "But you said it was good for you. You said—"

"I was lying!" I exclaim. "Because believe it or not, having your best friend declare that she doesn't want to be your best friend anymore kind of makes you feel like crap and I didn't want to guilt you into changing your mind because then I'd have to spend forever wondering if you actually wanted to spend time with me."

"Oh," she says. "I'm... I do. That's why I kept trying to... I do."

I throw back my head and sigh. "You're the worst. I love you so much, but you're the worst."

She pivots to face me. "Can we please be friends again?"

I roll my eyes. "I thought we'd already—"

"Can we please be friends again?" She repeats. "Because I've been sad and miserable and I've missed you like crazy and I don't know how I thought I'd make it even longer than this without you and I really, really need us to be friends again."

I smile. "Yes. We can... we can definitely do that."

She taps her heels against the floor and grins, rifling through her purse.

"What are—"

"Here," she hands me a HunGum. "This feels oath worthy."

Her expression falls when I just stare at it.

"We don't have to," she adds. "I know last time—"

"He doesn't sell them anymore."

She nods. "I know. Hear you got the last ones. We'll just have to make the next few really count then, right? I still have a pretty big stockpile anyway."

I pull off the wrapper and carefully hold it between my thumb and forefinger to keep it from getting stuck.

"I promise," she declares, holding out a finger. "to stop being an idiot or else all of my candy and toys will immediately go to Corrina Isabella Murphy."

"That might be a pretty difficult one to keep."

She rolls her eyes. "And you have to promise to tell me, okay? Next time I'm being stupid or making you mad or sad or... I want to say I'm going to get better at noticing, Cory, and I'm obviously going to try, but I might not. So if I'm going to stop being stupid, I need you to stop trying to hide that from me because otherwise I might not notice it's happening."

I nod and link my finger through hers. "I promise to tell Marnie next time she's being an idiot or else all of my candy and toys will immediately go to Marina Accardi."

We pop the HunGums between our teeth, repeat our oaths, and then, finally, we're back.

Chapter 26

We sit out there talking until it's time to go back in. And it's awkward, at first. Stilted. But the more we talk, the more we work our way back towards feeling right again. It doesn't take long. I've always fit in better right beside Marnie than anywhere else on any continent. So, when the music dies down and I try to pull her up with me and she stays seated, I'm confused.

"That's probably dinner," I say. "We should—"

"I might go home now, actually."

"Oh," I say. "Totally fine."

She smiles, but it doesn't reach her eyes. "Stay, Cory. Please."

I shake my head. "I literally only came because I thought you wanted to. Promise this is a milestone that I'm perfectly fine with missing, I barely even like anyone else in there."

"Liar. Go back in. Talk to him. Then... come gossip with me about it after?"

I roll my eyes. "Gabe's just a friend."

"A friend I caught staring at you for thirty minute straight? Sure."

I look away.

"Oh my god!" She slams her palms against the ground. "I'm right. Your whole face went red, I'm so, so, right." She gets to her feet just to accuse me more effectively.

"He doesn't like me back," I mumble.

She rolls her eyes. "Sure."

"I'm..." I sigh. "I know we thought... I get that he f-ed up big time and he knows that he f-ed up big time, but—"

"Hey," Marnie pressed her forehead to mine. "I trust your taste in humans, okay? I might question it sometimes, but I trust it."

"You can't get home on your own," I realize. "You barely got here, even with help. I should—"

"I texted my mom like fifteen minutes ago. She's probably already parked out front."

"When... you told me you were taking pictures!"

"I was," she shrugs. "I was just also texting her. I knew if I gave you too much of a heads up you'd come up with an excuse not to go talk to him."

I sigh. "I love you."

"Yeah, I know." She leans forward and my heartrate doesn't pick up. She licks her index finger and rubs at my forehead. "Foundation," she says. "A bit of mine came off on you. You're all good now."

I nod. My chest isn't even tight. It's just warm.

"I'll see you at home, okay?" She smiles. "Have so much fun. That's an order."

She leaves me there and it doesn't break me. My head isn't pulsing where she touched it.

I love Marina Accardi more than anyone else on the planet and right now, at least for today, that feels a lot more important than being in love with her.

Chapter 27

"Wow you look like, so lame right now."

I look up as Gabe slides into the empty seat beside me. Almost instantly. Because maybe, for some reason, he really was watching me. "Probably shouldn't be insulting people when they're holding knives," I point out.

He shrugs, picking up the one that was supposed to belong to Marnie. "Looks like I have one too now."

"Your friends probably think you're pretty lame too, you know. Chasing after some girl who wouldn't even agree to be you date?"

He twirls the knife between his fingers. "I'm just here to steal a second meal. This has nothing to do with you."

"Sure."

He leans towards me and drops his voice as if the twelfth graders we're sitting with have any interest in random grade nine drama. "You okay?" He asks. "Did she—"

"Dances have never really been Marnie's thing," I shrug. "We're good. We're... the good-est we've been for a while, actually. I think."

Gabe nods. "Good for you." He cuts into his porkchop. "Does that ummm... mean we're about to stop being goodish? Because I'd rather not. Do that."

"Oh my god," I grin. "You totally like me. How embarrassing."

He looks down. Whether it's to avoid looking at me or to aim better when he kicks my foot under the table, I'm unsure. "Shut up or I'll take it back."

I laugh. "We're still goodish too," I promise. "Marnie's the one who practically ordered me to stay and hangout with you, actually."

"Which you... didn't do."

I shrug. "I couldn't look like the clingy one." And the thought of walking up to him kept turning my legs to jelly, but he doesn't need to know that.

"I'm Marnie approved then?" He double checks.

"I still don't think she necessarily likes you," I admit. "But pretty much anyone who makes me happy would be Marnie approved. She's a nicer person than me."

He grins.

"What?" I sigh. "Now what did I—"

"You said I make you happy."

"I..." Apparently, my entire face goes noticeably red when I'm embarrassed about Gabe. I'll have to figure out how to stop landing myself in these kinds of situation around him. "Shut up!" I shove his shoulder.

He laughs.

"Marnie's gone all break anyway. Her mom and her sister take turns visiting each other. So, we have to be goodish because I'll still need someone to keep me entertained these next two weeks."

"And we're straight back to fake excuses."

I sigh. "Fine. No excuses? I... want to keep hanging out. Ish."

Gabe grins. "No excuses?" He puts the knife down and leans towards me to whisper, "I actually don't even like pork."

Chapter 28

I'm in my room texting Marnie when Mom yells, "your boy's here!"

I like that. I won't tell her that I like it because she's definitely doing it to annoy both of us, but it feels good to feel like the kind of girl that boys like Gabe can belong to.

"Tell him he can text before coming over next time!"

"I did!"

I smile to myself and roll my way out of bed. I try to quickly fix my hair in the mirror, but it just makes it stick out more.

"Hey," I find him by the front door. He's still in all of his snow gear.

"We're going sledding," he declares. "Get dressed."

"Gabe. You're fourteen."

"And you're boring. Hurry up, can't let some seven year old steal our spot."

I roll my eyes and open the closet.

"So," Gabe asks as we walk. There's a sledding hill a street over from our building, but everywhere always feels so much further in the snow. "You ready for the drama end-of-semester performance?"

I roll my eyes. We're all just performing our scripts again with 'all the new insight we've gained'. I think Mr. McCoy just assumes he's magically bettered us all as people through his random probing questions, but that's just how I've learned about some of the more boring bits of Gabe that I've been collecting recently. "Already have it memorized and everything."

"Nice. We've got it in the bag."

I sigh. "Drama's quite possibly the most useless class I've ever taken."

Gabe shrugs. "At least we'll have more time to study for other stuff. If... when does Marnie get back?"

I smile, kicking his boot. "Stop doing that."

"Stop doing what?"

"I promise I'm still fully planning on exploiting your abilities to somehow make sense of the French language even after Marnie's back, okay? I'll just be extra smart."

"I wasn't worried about that," he mumbles.

"Liar. You wouldn't bring her up that much if you weren't. Unless..." I falter. "You know Marnie like girls, right? Like, only likes—"

He rolls his eyes. "Believe me. I'm incredibly aware."

"Do you like her?" I don't know how I'd forgotten. Maybe years of 'you'd be so cute together' can rub off on a person. "Have you always—"

"Seriously, Cory?"

"What?"

Gabe sighs. "Nothing. No, I've never had a crush on Marnie."

"Never?"

He shrugs. "I mean, she's nice, nothing against her, I just haven't."

I nod.

"What about you? Any secret crushes I should know about."

"I..." we finally reach the hill. "Oh, shoot. Better go before it's too crowded!" I speed up.

"Very mature," Gabe jogs to catch back up with me.

I shrug. "I have no idea what you're talking about."

We sled until long after I've lost all feeling in my fingers and toes. That's for the best anyway. Gabe only brought one sled and I don't have one anymore so every time we crash (which ends up being a lot) he gets far too close for comfort. It's nice being physically too cold to have to worry about overheating. We walk to Tim Horton's afterward to try and dethaw our bodies with hot chocolate.

"So," Gabe hands me my cup and slides my debit card across the table where I'm guarding his sled. Because at some point, I've decided that I trust him enough to just hand that over. "Thing you're most and least excited for in 2016. Go."

I roll my eyes. "We don't have homework over the break."

"Maybe I'm just curious."

I think about it. "Least excited for the end of semester and final exams, most excited to get back to normal with Marnie."

"See, it's when you say stuff like that that a guy kinda starts to feel replaceable."

"You asked!" I exclaim. "You have other friends and you don't see me getting all jealous. I'm allowed to be social too, you know."

"Well then, my worst's also exams, my best is also you hanging out more with Marnie. I'll finally have more time to myself."

I stomp on his foot. "Asshole."

He smiles against his cup.

"Your real answer's camp starting up again, by the way," I inform him.

"I..." he considers. "Okay, yeah probably."

I beam. I know this boy. I like that I finally get to celebrate how well I know this boy.

So I'll learn to be okay with being friends. I managed with Marnie, so I'll do it again. Hopefully it just doesn't take as long this time.

Chapter 29

January's chaotic, but in a good way. Instead of having one exam per class worth thirty percent, we have one worth ten in January and then another worth twenty in May so we're not at a massive disadvantage compared to the schools with two completely separate terms. It's only ten percent, but they're also the first exams any of us have ever written, so everyone goes a bit crazy studying.

Luckily for me, I've managed to befriend two incredibly smart "I swear explaining things to you painfully slowly over and over again helps me study too" people, so I feel extra prepared in the days leading up to them. I think that's my type. That and partial Italians, apparently.

I've been dreading our drama end of term project (not because its difficult, but because I don't know how to do that without feeling like an idiot) but even that's relatively painless. Other groups are still crying and screaming and somehow going through whole life stories over the course of the two minutes we're on the stage. All Gabe and I come up with is an increasingly more angry set of 'hi's, but it turns out that that doesn't even matter because once everyone finishes, Mr. McCoy gets back on stage and claps to get our attention.

"Everyone," he pauses for dramatic effect. "Gets one hundred."

We start to cheer, but he silences us with a single finger.

"But," he continues. "I'll be expecting much more from your final project. True art cannot happen on a deadline so anytime from the beginning to the end of next semester, you may elect to show me your final product. After that, you're free to go. I won't mark anyone absent if you've already finished your performance so use the time to be inspired, make art, sleep in, whatever you want. But you've only got one shot at this. Don't waste it."

I'm already fully intending on wasting it.

Then come actual exams which I'm pretty sure I don't sweep with full one hundreds, but they also feel surprisingly fine. I'll have to start falling for nerds more often.

But mostly, I spend January finding (and refinding) my balance with my people. It still feels too big reintroducing Marnie and Gabe to each other, but I learn how to take rides to school with him (it actually stresses out Marnie a whole lot less when she doesn't have to count on me being on time every morning) and deny rides home so I can walk with Marnie every day except Fridays. I start to learn to navigate how to love her without being in love with her and liking him while acknowledging that I might be falling a little bit in love with him. Soon, I'm sure I'll perfect liking them both platonically.

Then, while I'm celebrating the last Sunday of freedom before semester two starts, Gabe ruins all of my carefully constructed plans.

Chapter 30

>*asshole: Can we go 4 a walk?*
>*me: its like 7pm*
>*me: and winter*
>*asshole: My mom can drive us to tims then. I'll tell her we have work to get done*
>*me: just come here?*
>*asshole: Ur mom home?*
>*me: yeah*
>*asshole: I'd really rather do tims*
>*asshole: Pleeeeeeeeeeeeeeeeeeeeeeaaaaaaaaaaaase*

I sigh, send a keyboard smash, and he knows me well enough to get his mom to pull up in front of me in the parking garage a few minutes later.

"I can't believe your drama teacher's giving you work to do before the semester's even started!" Mrs. DeLuca says. "She must hate kids."

Gabe squeezes the side of my thigh at the incorrect pronoun as if I've somehow been body-swapped with someone with half a braincell. As if that won't definitely also look suspicious.

"You know," I give her a tight-lipped smile and gesture vaguely. "Theatre people. Show must always go on."

She drops us off in front of Tim Hortons and even though he was the one who insisted I come, Gabe leaves me on the sidewalk and darts inside. I shove my numbing fingers into my pockets and follow. "What's up?" I find him physically bouncing with energy in line. I've been visiting coffee shops with him all semester, so I know for a fact he doesn't drink coffee but I'm suddenly unconvinced.

"Want something to drink?" He asks. "Or eat? I can pay. Anything you want."

"Hmmm well in that case, fifty cinnamon rolls please."

"Okay."

I frown. "Gabe, I was joking. Are you even listening to me?"

He laughs and rolls his eyes. "Obviously I was just gonna get you one. Go save us a table."

It's practically empty because it's a suburban Tim Horton's after 7pm, but I grab one anyway.

Gabe sits down across from me and hands me my cinnamon bun, but he never actually stops being in motion. I'm pretty sure his legs are already bouncing before he's even finished lowering himself into the chair. He's not just nervous, he's terrified. And suddenly, I am too.

"Hey," I reach across the table to touch his arm. Press my foot against the side of his to try and stop it from shaking. "Are you okay? Did something happen?"

He laughs again. I don't know how I didn't notice how breathy it was the first time. "I'm fine."

"You don't seem fine." I pull my chair closer and lean as far forward as I can. "If something happened, we'll—"

His eyebrows shoot up. "I'm fine," he says, a bit calmer this time. "I promise. I umm..." he pulls his backpack up onto his lap and takes out his laptop. "I was thinking about drama? We said we're presenting immediately, right? Like, tomorrow, if he'll let us?"

"Oh absolutely."

"I thought we should go over our answers." He taps against the side of his computer as it powers up.

I frown. "The ones that had absolutely no impact on how we decided to say the same word over and over again?"

Gabe's ears go red. "I don't know, he's a teacher, right? And he seems pretty sure they'd help. Might be worth it."

"If it's freaking you out this much, we don't have to present tomorrow. I'm..." I sigh. "Willing to wake up at 7am a few more times if you need me to," I admit. "But only for like, a few weeks." He doesn't need to know that I'd keep going to the class until the last day of the semester if he asked me to.

"No," he shakes his head. "Definitely want to get it over with. Just... read the stupid thing?"

I roll my eyes. "I've intentionally been avoiding a few of your answers."

"The questions then," he suggests. "I can make one with just the questions so we can answer them again and—"

"Gabe." I slowly push the laptop shut. "Believe it or not, I'm kind of past needing a script and prompts to talk to you."

He sighs. "Just read the questions."

"No."

"Just—"

"Not until you tell me what's going on."

"Just—"

"No!"

"I'm trying to ask you out, you idiot!" Gabe freezes, looking around. The few customers remaining don't seem as invested in us as he's convinced himself that they are.

"I'm... what?" I try and fail and try again to fight down a smile.

He picks at his donut. "Nothing."

"No, no, I'm sorry. What was that?"

He sighs. "Maybe I was trying to ask you out, okay?"

"Hmmm," my heart is fluttering and my head is soaring but I need to be cool here. This is my once chance to be incredibly cool. "I hear that normally doesn't involve calling the other person an idiot."

He blushes. "Yeah, that part was... probably inadvisable."

I smile. "Do it again. Promise I'll play along this time."

"Are you going to say yes or is this some weird new torture technique you're trying out?"

"Guess you'll have to find out."

He looks back at his donut.

"Gabe," I tap his foot with mine. "Yes, okay? Walk me through it anyway? I'm usually not the one who gets to actually be asked out."

He smiles a bit, reopening the laptop and spinning it to face me. "So you were going to get to the bottom, right? And you could've read anything along the way and it wouldn't have mattered because if anything it's just more proof that I like you but then you get to the end and I added something like 'hi Cory, I like you. Can I take you on a date sometime?' and you were supposed to be all surprised and be the embarrassed one, by the way. So thanks for ruining that, I guess."

I laugh. I can't help myself.

"Well," he closes the laptop. "I guess that's—"

"No!" I catch his hand. "No, I... I'm sorry. That's just a really bad way to ask someone out."

"Shut up," he rolls his eyes.

"Hi Cory, I like you? You had enough time to think it out and write it down and you decided to go with 'hi Cory, I like you'?"

"Okay, for the record, English is absolutely my worst subject. I was trying to be all sweet though. You don't have to—"

I take his other hand. I look him straight in the eye. Brown, like chestnuts.

"Hi Gabe," I say slowly. "I like you too."

His lips tremble and then he's laughing too.

"See!" I swat his arm. "Awful. Terrible. Really sweet, but awful." I swallow. I know we have to get serious, but I'm suddenly scared to. "Just to double... you're serious?"

"In what world would I put myself through this for a bit?"

"Believe it or not, I've been asked out as a part of quite a few of those. And then all of the sudden on some random Sunday you decide you desperately have to—"

Gabe sighs. "Cory, it's the second time I've tried asking."

"I... what?"

"I asked you to semi?" He reminds me. "And you instantly started pretending I didn't like girls?"

I blush. "I didn't mean to... I didn't think you liked me, not girls as a whole. I... there's no way that was you asking me out! That wouldn't been such an awful way to do it."

"Yeah, and we've established that's something I'm kind of awful at."

"You're serious?" I triple check.

"I'm serious. But if you don't like me back, no I'm not and this was all just an end of semester joke."

"I'm pretty sure I've liked you for a few months now," I admit.

He buries his face in his hands, raking his fingers through his hair. "Oh thank god, that would've been so, so, embarrassing. I umm... actually didn't formally plan a date or anything yet? I just didn't want to wait another semester before—"

It's too much of a reminder of what I'd meant to do with her. I frown. He notices me frowning.

"Hey." He points at me. "No taking it back."

I sigh. "I really like you. I just... I think I need to check with Marnie, first? We just started figuring things out and I can't..."

Gabe frowns. "I know you trust Marnie, but I can't... I barely know her. I don't think I'd be ready to—"

"No, of course not," I stop him. "Obviously. That was just if we were pretending. I'm..." I swallow. "I really, really, want to say yes and I'm not still like, randomly holding a grudge from sixth grade, but it would also be fair if she still was? And I'm..." I can feel my eyes starting to water, but I refuse to cry in a Tim Hortons. "We've only started tolerating each other a few months ago and I really, really, like you, but she's been the most important person in my life forever and if this is going to—"

"Talk to her. Let me know how it goes. I told my mom not to go too far so she's probably still outside if you want to go right now."

I hesitate. "This has nothing to do with how much I like you, yeah? With anyone, I'd—"

"Cory." He pats my arm. "It's okay. Talk to her. Just... if she's not okay with it can we pretend that this never happened?"

I try to smile, but I can already feel it wavering.

"Deal," I whisper.

Chapter 31

I plan out how to tell her the whole ride home. I go over dozens of possible questions and reactions. But nothing would have prepared me to find her sitting outside my door, waiting for me.

"Oh, hey," I stumble. "What are—"

"Can we talk?"

"Sure? I actually had to talk to you too." I reach for my keys, but she grabs my arm. "Out here?"

"Sure?" I sit down.

"Here's the plan," she says. "I'm going to stare at that wall and you're also going to stare at that wall until I'm finished because otherwise I don't think I'll say it."

I nod. I focus my eyes. "Ready."

"I'm... when I was being stupid in September you asked if Izzie said I couldn't talk to you, right? And I said no which was true but... maybe she should have? Because I didn't just... I didn't only think we needed space because I wanted to find myself or let you find yourself or whatever. I'm... I've had a crush on you for years, Cory."

All the oxygen in my chest freezes.

No. No, no, no, no, no, no.

Movies make being liked by multiple people seem fun and exciting but somehow, I feel like I've gone from having one really good option to none at all.

"And this isn't me asking you out," she's still going. "I know you're straight. I just... I really don't want to mess up another semester and I think trying to hide it's been part of the problem? I'm trying to get over it, I swear, but I—" She stops. "You're crying, Cory."

I wipe at my face. "Am not," I lie.

"Hey," she wraps her arm around my shoulders. "It's okay, alright? We're okay. I love you so, so, much. I'm also a little in love with you but that's... you're not letting me down, alright?

You could never. I've always known that it was never an actual option."

I'm supposed to tell her that I'm bi, but I can't. I don't even think I'd be ashamed of it, but I physically can't say it. "I was coming to find you," I whisper instead. "Gabe just asked me out. I was coming to—"

"Oh," she jolts. "Oh my god. That's... I'm fine, okay? I promise I'm fine."

"I could say no? That's why I wanted to talk. To make sure... if that'll be hard for you, I can say no. He'd understand too. I told him I had to talk to you first so we—"

"Hey." She adjusts. Knees against knees, forehead to forehead. "I've been waiting for you guys to figure that out for way too long for you to throw it away just because I decided to tell you at the worst possible moment, okay? Do it. You obviously like him back. This can just be a really funny maid of honour speech for me to give at your wedding."

I laugh. "I love you," I say. "So much."

She smiles even though her eyes are also shining, wiping a tear off her cheek. "You too, okay? Forever." She takes a deep breath and stands up. "He's better now?" She double checks. "He's good enough for you?"

"I'm..." I think about it. "I think so? I think he might make me feel really great about being me."

"Then go apologize for thinking it was at all okay to consult a friend before telling him that."

I laugh. "Will do."

I manage to get all the way back into the stairwell before breaking down.

Chapter 32

"Hey," Gabe sits down beside me.

I sigh and try to dry my face. "Dang it, now you've seen me cry more."

"You're the one who summoned me."

I look down at my phone. Oh. So I had. "You were supposed to be slower."

I take a long breath. Let it go.

"I need to tell you something," I decide. "But I don't know if it's an okay thing to talk about in the building."

He stands up and holds out a hand. "Come on. Let's go up a few floors where everyone's too rich to know anything about either of us."

We loop around and around the seventh floor while I try to unstick my throat. His hand doesn't leave mine. And it feels... not as right as Marnie's, but more exciting than Marnie's. A bit too hot. A little electric.

Eventually, Gabe sighs. "Promise I won't be like, absolutely heartbroken," he says. "I'm actually really cool and tough."

I roll my eyes. "I still want to try dating."

"Oh," he smiles a bit. "Cool. Good to know. Why are you—"

"Marnie likes me," I blurt. "She just told me."

"Dang it, really thought I was beating her to that."

I frown. "You knew?"

"Cory, I'm pretty sure everyone knows."

"I don't like her back," I quickly explain. "And we have her blessing and everything or whatever, I think I was just... she said she just needed me to know? And I have liked her, I think or know or... something but for some reason I still couldn't get myself to even tell her that I like girls and..." I sigh. "You're supposed to act more surprised about that, you know."

"Right," his ears go red. "Sorry. I'm just... in so much shock that I forgot to express it?"

I hit his shoulder.

"Girls and guys though, right?" He checks. "Just so we're super clear."

I nod. "Girls and guys, I think. But no one else knows yet, so..."

Gabe shrugs. "Same."

I sigh, turning to look at him. "Does it feel like cheating, sometimes?" I ask. "Liking girls? Or like you're betraying someone but you don't even know who because that part gets to be easy and open and—"

"Yeah," he admits. "Doesn't mean it's any less... I do like you," he says. "You just happen to be the more convenient gender to like, but I wouldn't have asked you out if I didn't actually like you."

I make myself meet his eye. Just for a moment. "Same." I swallow. "Marnie would be so fine with knowing, obviously. And our moms. Which I know I'm super lucky about obviously and I'm not trying to brag or—"

"You're fine."

"Right. She'd be so fine with it and so would everyone else who really matters but I think that's why they can't know? Because I've known. Maybe not specific labels or anything, but I've at least known that I liked her for practically ever and I still let her be out by herself for years."

Gabe squeezes my hand. "Different people need different amounts of time."

"I know."

"She's not going to be mad, you know. If you ever do tell her."

"I know. That's why I should..." I sigh. "I don't know. I don't know what I'm doing." I catch myself. "I want to do this though. I want to try us. I know it's not exactly a vote of confidence that I'm crying about the last girl I liked less than an hour after you asked me out, but I swear I really do."

He laughs a little. "Good to know."

"I just needed you to know that I'm always going to be... a lot about her, I guess? Not because I like her like that anymore because I'm pretty sure I don't right now, but I'm... it's messy."

He rolls his eyes. "Cory, I was half expecting to ask you out only to find out that you and Marnie have been secretly dating for years. It's fine. I've always known you were a mess."

I try to stomp on his foot but he jumps away, laughing.

"I got you a thing actually," he says. "Not as a 'please go out with me' bribe, I'm not that desperate. I was supposed to be for after we finished the drama thing so now you'll just have to pretend I gave it to you tomorrow."

"Oh. Thanks?"

"Unless you want to wait. Maybe we should—"

I roll my eyes. "You can't just tell someone you got them a gift then make them wait for it, asshole."

He unzips his backpack and tosses a bag at me. "Here."

I open it. Gasp. "Gabe."

"Oh, thank god. Fully thought you'd already bought some," he rambles.

"Gabe."

"They're actually super easy to find online? Just took a while to ship but full disclosure, they came in a few weeks ago but I couldn't think of a non-awkward time to—"

"You should have given them to me before I talked to Marnie!" I exclaim. "Then she definitely would have—"

He shrugs. "Didn't really feel like bribing her with gross looking caramel candies."

I laugh. I think I'd cry if I didn't. And then, I'm suddenly the me that I got to be in middle school again. I rediscover how to make the first move. I step forward, throw my arms around the neck, and kiss Gabe DeLuca on the seventh floor.

Nonymous

Maybe the altitude's messing with both of our heads, because he kisses me back.

Chapter 33

"Hi."

    "Hi."

      "Hi."

        "Hi."

          "Hi."

            "Hi."

              "Hi."

                "Hi."

                  "Hi."

                    "Hi."

                      "Hi."

Mr. McCoy calls us into his office at lunch and for a moment, I'm worried we've miscalculated. Our performance barely counted as a performance. It was even less emotional than any of the times we'd had to rerun the script in class. Just as monotone as the first time we read it. We'd be banking on him not wanting to risk giving anyone a bad enough grade to justify talking to the school about how far from the other drama classes he was straying. But then he asks us to sit down.

    On the floor, of course. There are no chairs in his office.

    "Corrina," he says. "Gabriel. Can I swear the two of you to secrecy?"

    We look at each other, shrug, and nod.

    "I'm giving you both 100."

    My eyes go wide. I'm pretty sure I hear Gabe make a choking sound. We were counting on at least a B- by default, but definitely not that. Neither of us have any business being in a drama class.

    Mr. McCoy smiles at our surprise and I realize that maybe that's exactly why he's given us perfect.

"I loved your performance," he says. "It was different. Rebellious."

It had actually just been lazy, but neither of us correct him. "Don't lose that, okay? Never stop pushing back against the grain. Don't forget what you've learned here."

And then he tells us to have a good year, dismisses us, and that's it.

I think Mr. McCoy might be a little convinced that all of our lives revolved around him and his class. That the moment any of us walked through those theatre doors on that first day, our stories climactic finales were inevitably going to be sitting across from him on his office floor, waiting to hear whatever final piece of wisdom he had to bestow. Maybe for some people, it will be. I've been too caught up in my own life to really focus on anyone else in that class. Maybe he really has changed a few lives for the better and they'll give him the dramatic finale he's looking for.

I leave that office trying my best to look thoughtful and reflective for his sake, grab Gabe's hand the moment we're out of view, and run down the hall so we can both burst out laughing a polite distance away.

This isn't our ending yet. Not even a little bit.

Nonymous

Nonymous

Acknowledgement & About the Author

Thanks as always to all of my early readers for the help with this one. Specifically L. Brennan, Onyx Kotzma, R. Burwell, El H., and Katie B.! You're all amazing.

Alex (any pronouns, feel free to talk about me behind my back at will I'm impossible to mispronoun) published their first book after turning 20, promptly decided to publish a book a month those next ten months because that was reasonable, and is now trying to hit 22 before turning 22 because he has no concept of time. To join her reading list and get 1 email a month with info on new and upcoming releases, early reader opportunities, genre polls, and other polls (Alex really likes polls), message them at alexnonymouswrites@gmail.com

See you next month :)

Printed in Great Britain
by Amazon